# SNOWED IN WITH MY BEST FRIEND

## A MONTGOMERY INK LEGACY ROMANCE

## CARRIE ANN RYAN

Snowed in with my Best Friend
By: Carrie Ann Ryan
© 2025 Carrie Ann Ryan

Cover Art by Insta Love Graphic Design

# PRAISE FOR CARRIE ANN RYAN

"Count on Carrie Ann Ryan for emotional, sexy, character driven stories that capture your heart!" – Carly Phillips, NY Times bestselling author

"Carrie Ann Ryan's romances are my newest addiction! The emotion in her books captures me from the very beginning. The hope and healing hold me close until the end. These love stories will simply sweep you away." ~ NYT Bestselling Author Deveny Perry

"Carrie Ann Ryan writes the perfect balance of sweet and heat ensuring every story feeds the soul." - Audrey Carlan, #1 New York Times Bestselling Author

"Carrie Ann Ryan never fails to draw readers in with passion, raw sensuality, and characters that pop off the page. Any book by Carrie Ann is an absolute treat." – New York Times Bestselling Author J. Kenner

"Carrie Ann Ryan knows how to pull your heart-strings and make your pulse pound! Her wonderful Redwood Pack series will draw you in and keep you reading long into the night. I can't wait to see what comes next with the new generation, the Talons. Keep them coming, Carrie Ann!" –Lara Adrian, New York Times bestselling author of CRAVE THE NIGHT

"With snarky humor, sizzling love scenes, and brilliant, imaginative worldbuilding, The Dante's Circle series reads as if Carrie Ann Ryan peeked at my personal wish list!" – NYT Bestselling Author, Larissa Ione

"Carrie Ann Ryan writes sexy shifters in a world full of passionate happily-ever-afters." – *New York Times* Bestselling Author Vivian Arend

"Carrie Ann's books are sexy with characters you can't help but love from page one. They are heat and heart blended to perfection." *New York Times* Best-selling Author Jayne Rylon

Carrie Ann Ryan's books are wickedly funny and deliciously hot, with plenty of twists to keep you guessing. They'll keep you up all night!" USA Today Bestselling Author Cari Quinn

"Once again, Carrie Ann Ryan knocks the Dante's Circle series out of the park. The queen of hot, sexy, enthralling paranormal romance, Carrie Ann is an author not to miss!" *New York Times* bestselling Author Marie Harte

# CHAPTER 1

## CULLEN

If there was one thing I knew about attending a Montgomery holiday party—or rather any of their events—it was that bringing cheese to the occasion would smooth the way of any awkward introductions or personalities.

Mostly because I *was* the awkward personality.

I looked down at the basket of cheese in my hand, and then at the red wine the lady behind the counter had said would match nicely with it. "Insanity is doing the same thing repeatedly and expecting it to have a different outcome."

"Are you talking to the cheese and wine or yourself?"

I looked over at my friend and boss, Lexington

Wilder Montgomery, and snorted. "Which would be the gentlest answer for you?"

Lex held out his hand and took the wine before giving me one of those deep hugs that we gave one-handed. "Good to see you, Cullen. I wasn't sure you were going to be able to make it."

I shrugged, feeling awkward once again. It was practically stamped on my forehead at this time. "I don't leave until tomorrow for my parents' house. And it's not like I had other invites."

"I don't know how I'm supposed to take that," Lex said with a laugh as we walked into the large home his parents had built. We were up in Fort Collins, rather than in Denver where I worked now, but honestly, with I-25 the way it was, everything was one big city.

I had started working for the family over twelve years ago now. Which seemed insane because I had to be only twenty-one, right? At least, that's what I told myself whenever I said I had plenty of time to settle down and figure out what I wanted for the rest of my life. Except I wasn't sure that was going to happen anytime soon. Not with the person I had on my mind, nor with anyone else for that matter.

A woman with a kind smile and bright eyes leaned forward. "Oh, you brought cheese, that's fantastic, thank you. Did you talk with Jessa at The Market?"

I didn't know which Montgomery had spoken other than I thought it was one of Lexington's aunts on the Fort Collins Montgomery side, but I still needed them to all wear name tags. It didn't help that a large number of the family members each held businesses of their own and invited their employees. So there had to be over a hundred people milling about inside and out, all laughing and eating and drinking and acting as if this was a normal occurrence.

Except with the Montgomerys it was.

I shouldn't feel too out of my element though, considering I had eight brothers and sisters. I was also the oldest and hadn't settled down yet.

Hence the next day's long drive up to the family ranch.

I cleared my throat. "You're welcome. Thank you for inviting me. And yes. I love the Market."

The older woman smiled, laughter in her eyes. I had to wonder if she could read the confusion on my face. "I'm Annabelle, by the way, Lexington's aunt. Not all of the siblings and cousins are here, so you don't have to be worried about being too overwhelmed."

"This is Cullen, Aunt Annabelle, you do realize that he has more siblings than you?"

She grinned then, her eyes brightening. "Oh yes, I remember that. We've met a few of them, right?"

I nodded, sticking my hands in my dark jeans pockets since I didn't know what to do with them.

I wasn't usually this antsy. In fact, I was usually the easygoing guy, who was good with his hands, could make any conversation, and was just the good guy. However, somebody that I was trying to keep off my mind was going to be here tonight, and I had to pretend that I was clearly not falling in love with her.

Because that made sense. After all, we were just friends, and I was fine with that. And I wasn't sure I'd be able to push down those feelings any longer. But I wasn't going to do anything to force her to want me. She didn't, and that was just going to have to be it. I would get over my feelings eventually.

"Cullen?" Annabelle asked. "Is everything okay?"

I cleared my throat. "Sorry. Wool gathering."

Understanding filled her gaze, though she was the only one who understood. I sure didn't. "Well, let's get you a drink and something to eat, then you can mill about. Do you know a few people? Or I can introduce you?"

Lex squeezed my shoulders. "It's okay, Aunt Annabelle, I can help Cullen here."

"No, you need to go fix *something*. You know what," she said. Whe narrowed her gaze at my boss, and Lex sighed.

"Okay, I'm throwing you to the wolves. Sorry." And with that, Lex scampered off into the crowd, and I lost him.

I blinked after him, confused. "What just happened?"

She rolled her eyes, though her smile was genuine. "Family. We're fun, but we're loud. Come on, let me show you around."

In the end, I met another six Montgomerys and found myself standing in a corner with Crew, who was engaged to Aria Montgomery, one of Lex's cousins, and Dash, who was also a cousin, but Lex's real cousin, and not a second cousin twice removed or something like that like most of these people were. I knew Crew because I had helped build a couple of his properties, considering I was the master plumber for Montgomery Construction, and I worked with Dash. The kid was over a decade younger than me, and yet we got along just fine. In fact, he was sometimes my boss on a few properties.

And thankfully, the Montgomerys didn't make it weird.

"I'm glad you came," Dash said as he grinned at me. That was Dash, always happy and bubbly and looking as if he had a few secrets to share. He also got shit done. He was the main foreman for Montgomery Construction, just like Lex was an architect.

They were an offshoot of Montgomery Builders, which was the Fort Collins branch, and Montgomery Inc., the Denver branch. Instead of the next generation trying to figure out which branch to join, they had just made their own, combining everything into one trust. I was still shocked that anybody could make all of that work, but if anyone could, it was this family.

"I'm glad I could come too. I brought cheese and wine."

"I suppose you've learned how to work with the Montgomerys after a decade," Crew said as he lifted his beer bottle to his lips.

My lips quirked into a smile. "I try. Although I swear these parties are getting bigger and bigger."

"People are getting married, and we're adding more staff that we actually like hanging out with."

"I'm going to take it as a good thing that you're saying it in front of me?" I asked, teasing.

Dash blushed. "Sorry. I mean, you've been working for my family longer than I have."

"Considering I don't think you were even in high school when I started working for the Montgomerys, albeit your uncle's company, yeah, probably."

"Oh yeah, I forgot that. Well, I bet Lex was glad to get you considering you're the guy who can pretty much do anything when it comes to plumbing."

"I should really put that on my business cards. Or my dating profile," I said dryly.

Dash's brows rose. "You're back on the apps? A glutton for punishment, are you?"

I mentally winced. "Not right now. They don't really work with the holidays. But eventually I'll get out there. Find someone."

"I'm sure this one has a cousin or four," Crew added, pointing his thumb over at Dash.

The younger man beamed. "*And* one that doesn't work with us. Plus, Lex has a whole other set of cousins that live in other states. I mean, we aren't as big as your family, but we're getting there."

"That statement scares me," Crew said dryly.

Honestly, the sibling and cousin math made my head hurt. "I may have more *siblings* than you do, but I think we have the same number as at least one of the generations in this group did. Either way, both of my parents each only had a single sibling and they didn't have kids, so it isn't like I have any cousins."

Dash put a hand over his chest, his face mock surprised. "No cousins? How does that work?"

"I'll tell you all about it when you're older," Crew said as he tipped back his beer. "And on that note, I see the person I was looking for."

Crew didn't even bother to acknowledge us as he pushed past us and set his beer bottle near the other empties. He grinned down at his fiancée as Aria beamed up at him. And he put both hands on her face and kissed her soundly on the mouth.

Some whistled, a few groaned, and another even threw a balled-up napkin.

"Whoever threw that better clean up after themselves!" a woman's voice shouted as the entire room broke out into laughter, her included.

I joined in before taking a sip of my beer. "You guys know to how to throw parties."

Dash began to talk about the project we were on, invested in the number of growing enterprises the Montgomerys were working on. I listened with half an ear, but I couldn't help but think about the one person who had been on my mind for far too long. We hadn't seen each other in forty-eight hours, which, considering Posy never left her house as she worked from home, it made sense. But I liked having coffee with her at Latte on the Rocks and going for walks because she had said we both needed the fresh air.

She told me she would be here as she and her friend Mercy had been invited by Lex's mom, so here I was, wondering again why I was stressing out about seeing a woman that I saw often.

Then the group parted, and I saw her.

I swallowed hard, trying not to choke on my beer as I studied the woman who had me up late at night. She wore a forest green dress that was straight across the collarbone, but otherwise sleeveless. It tucked in at the waist with a little belt, and it flared out past her knees. She had on red chunky heels, and gold and glittery jewelry. But it was her hair that always got me.

A luscious red that was all natural and matched those light blue eyes of hers. It fell in waves around her shoulders, and I tried to look away before she caught me staring. But from the way her lightly painted mouth curved into a smile, I wasn't going to be getting out of this without having to speak and lie to myself.

My phone buzzed in my pocket, and I pulled my gaze away, grateful for the interruption.

"Hey, it's my mom, I'm going to go take this outside so I can answer the video call."

"No problem, I'm going to go steal one of those mini tarts."

"I don't know if it's stealing if it's on the buffet."

"Oh no, I'm going to go steal it off of my sister's plate," he said with a laugh, and I just shook my head and watched the adult man go annoy his adult sister.

I moved to the back deck, down the stairs, and away from the crowd. I had missed the call because it had taken me so long to get through everyone that I knew, and I quickly hit the return call.

"There's my boy," Mom said as she grinned into the phone, Dad right beside her.

"Well, hi there. Sorry I didn't answer right away, I'm at the Montgomery party."

"They take such good care of you."

"They do. But don't worry, I'm ready to come to the other loud house with too many siblings that I love."

"I'm not sure how to take that, son," my dad said with a grin. "But you're doing well? Is your truck going to be okay for the drive? I know there's a storm heading out."

"The storm's not hitting until at least two in the morning, and I will be well tucked into my childhood bed by then."

"It's sweet you think that we have that for you since you're thirty-nine, my darling. We made that into a gym that we don't use long ago."

I rolled my eyes because she wasn't lying. "But yes, the truck's all ready to go and I'm packed. I'm going to like the drive. The trees are gorgeous until it's suddenly flat land."

"That's Wyoming for you," she teased.

We spoke for a few moments before I finally couldn't take the cold anymore, since I wasn't wearing a jacket, and said my goodbyes.

Shivering, and with my hands in my pockets, I went up the deck stairs and through the glass doors and nearly ran into Posy.

"Oh, Cullen, there you are. I thought I saw you earlier. Are you okay?"

I had reached out to steady both of us, and now my hands were on her elbows, and I swallowed hard, looking down at the woman who was just my friend.

"Yeah, I was just talking to Mom and Dad."

"Oh, you're visiting them soon, right?"

"Tomorrow," I said and quickly lowered my

hands because I realized I was still touching her. "It's good to see you here."

Her lips tilted. "You mean out of my house? Don't worry, I plan on having a good time and then making the drive to my parents' house tomorrow. Leaving the house two days in a row. How about that."

"You know, that deserves a reward. Maybe a piece of cheese."

"You've already been assimilated into the group I see."

"Are you going to be okay driving alone tomorrow? How long of a drive do you have? You know there's a storm coming, right?"

She shook her head, a smile playing on her lips. "You sound just like my dad. But no, I'll be at my house long before the storm hits."

I frowned and remembered where she had said her parents lived. "You're right. It's just beyond my parents' place, so you should make it as long as you head out early."

"Thanks for the permission. Don't worry, I'll be fine. I know how to drive up there. I wish there was an easier way to fly, but in the end, you're just circling the area and it takes longer."

"Exactly," I said, sliding my hands into my pockets.

"Oh look, we snagged another," a voice said.

"And they're not related," a deeper voice called out.

I frowned as everyone stared at us before a creeping sensation slid up my neck.

I looked down at Posy, who at first went pale before her cheeks pinkened, and I couldn't help but look up.

"You really put mistletoe at a family party?" I asked, with a sigh.

"That was Riley, blame her!" a woman called out, and I just shook my head and looked down at Posy.

"I'll create a distraction if you want to run for it."

She rolled her eyes. "Just kiss me, already. I believe they're already starting to chant."

"Kiss! Kiss! Kiss! Kiss!"

I sighed, annoyed, and yet, maybe not. This was just a fun thing to do. We could still remain friends afterwards, and it wouldn't be weird. So when I lowered my face to hers, and she went up to her tiptoes, I tried to look as if this were a natural thing. As if we'd done it a thousand times. Her lips brushed against mine softly, and I wanted to lean forward and ask for more. But then she was two steps away, eyes wide, as everybody moved forward, giving me hugs or tapping me on the back, laughing it off as if I hadn't just kissed the woman that I called friend, and the woman who I wanted more than anything.

But I was thirty-nine years old. It wasn't as if kissing a woman was new to me.

But this wasn't like one of those movies where mistletoe grew out of the ceiling and suddenly light burst around you and that kiss turned into something more. A deep and abiding connection that changed the game.

Instead, she had kissed the side of my mouth, mostly my big beard, and then stepped away as if I had shocked her.

And now I couldn't find her in the crowd.

That was for the best. I would say goodbye to her on my way out, if I could find her, and we would remain friends. Because Posy needed friends. And as I watched all of the people in my life fall in love and start families, the one thing that I desperately wanted to do, I figured it was time to maybe take a step back and figure out exactly how to survive in a world where everybody was moving along, I wasn't.

I stayed at the party for another couple of hours, only having one beer and switching to sparkling water soon after, and honestly had a great time. I grabbed my jacket from the coat room and shivered my way down to my truck, grateful that this property was on so much land that they had enough space for all of the vehicles. The Montgomerys did not play when it came to drinking and driving, so there were already rideshares and a rented bus to get people about.

I saluted to Crew and Aria as they made their way out, and was two cars away from my truck when I saw a familiar beat-up sedan.

The engine whirled for a moment, then choked, whirled again, and choked once more. And then nothing.

I moved forward, cursing under my breath as I tapped the window.

Posy's scream would've fit in any horror movie, and I winced.

"You okay?" I asked through the window.

She gestured for me to move back as she opened the door and stomped her feet when she got out.

"Sorry for screaming. It's dark, and well, you could have been an ax murderer."

"I promise I left my ax at home." I pause. "Or maybe in the back of the truck. I don't really remember. I would ask if your car's okay, but we both heard what was going on."

She sighed. "I don't know cars, but it sounds like something is wrong. I know that there's got to be a mechanic in that house, because there're so many people and it just makes sense statistically, but I'm cold, and now I have no idea how I'm going to get to my parents' house. I just had this car looked at."

I looked down at the sedan, at its worn tires, and shook my head. "I thought you were getting a new car, Posy."

"I was. And then I needed a new water heater. And part of a new roof when the tornadoes that Colorado said they never get came in. So insurance gave me the runaround. I was planning on buying a car in the new year, that way I could get last year's model and save some money, but that doesn't really help me right now because I'm cold, and now I'm going to have to cancel going to my parents'."

"I can help with the cold thing, and fuck, I can help with the parent thing."

Her brows rose. "What?"

"Get in my truck, I'll drive you home. And then, I'll drive you to your parents. We're going the same way, and I'm not going to have you sit alone in your house for the holidays because of your damn car. We will get it fixed."

"Cullen, you don't have to do that."

"I don't. But I want to. We're friends, Posy. It's what we do. Let me help you."

"It's out of your way."

"Not that far. And I don't mind. But I think my toes are about to freeze, and probably other parts of me, so let's get in the truck."

She burst out laughing, even though she kept shaking her head.

"It's too much."

"It's not. Let's grab anything you need out of your car, and we'll deal with it tomorrow. It's going to be okay, Posy. I promise."

She gave me a look that said she didn't quite believe me, but when I held up my hand and she took it, I thought that maybe, just maybe, I hadn't quite been lying.

I just had to make sure I didn't fall for the woman who was slowly becoming my best friend. Easy.

# CHAPTER 2

POSY

*I* lowered my hands from my lips and let out a breath. This wasn't the first time I'd done that motion, and it was beginning to be a problem.

Once again, I needed to stop thinking about that kiss. I had been tossing and turning all night, so now not even the best concealer could hide the dark circles under my eyes. I was doing my best though, because I couldn't let Cullen see how he had affected me.

Of course, I could just lie and say I was stressed about the drive, the fact that my car was probably dead for good, and countless other things, but I didn't really know how I was supposed to explain that.

I went through my packing list again, ensuring that I was taking up the least amount of space as possible. I knew that Cullen had a huge truck and there was probably enough room for more than a tiny suitcase, but for all I knew he had enough gifts for all of his siblings, and I was going to have to sit on my purse or something.

I ran my hands over my face, avoiding my lips, before I began to pace my bedroom again.

I wasn't sure why I was acting like this. It was just a kiss under the mistletoe, and yes, I had practically jumped away in terror, but it wasn't like it was his fault. He didn't do it on purpose.

I had been the one to meet him underneath the mistletoe so maybe all of this was my fault rather than his.

He probably wasn't even thinking about the kiss.

My phone buzzed, and I immediately snatched it, grateful for something else to think about. "Mercy! How is everything? Did you have fun at the party last night?"

"I did." There was something odd in her tone, but she didn't clarify what she meant.

"I just wanted to make sure you got home safe, but it was late so I didn't text. Didn't want to push that text through your Do Not Disturb."

"Everything went well. I'm glad I got to go. The Montgomerys are so nice."

"You grew up with them, right?" I asked, trying to remember exactly how she was connected to them.

"I did. Lex and I have known each other forever. And well, now he's my neighbor, so I guess the Montgomerys are always going to be around."

"Are you all set for your Christmas day?" I asked, feeling bad that she couldn't come with me. She had already declined multiple times when I had offered, and now I didn't even have a car to get her there.

"I'll be okay. You have fun with your parents."

"I will. I love seeing them."

"Tell them 'Hi' for me. Your car going to make it there okay?"

I wince. "Not exactly." I explained the whole situation from the night before, and exactly how I was getting to my parents' home.

Mercy grinned. "That's so sweet of Cullen. I'm glad that you're going to make it work out."

"Hey, Mercy, when I'm back in town after the new year, do you want to help me buy a car?" I didn't want to think about my budget in that moment, but I couldn't help it. This was *not* the time for this.

"Sure! And we can totally work on our badass looks so we can stare down any salesmen who think we need a man in order to make it happen." Mercy rocked back on her heels, grinning.

"I'm glad I have you for that, because we both know I'm going to cower behind a pole."

"You wouldn't. But I can kick ass." She held up both fists, play fighting.

"Damn straight," I said with a laugh.

"Merry Christmas and happy holidays, Mercy."

"Same to you. Enjoy your time and tell me all about this car trip with Cullen."

I ignored the teasing in her tone, because frankly one of us needed to. "He's my friend. Just like you and Lex are friends."

"That makes sense," she said quickly. Too quickly.

And now I had way too many questions, but not enough time. "I need to head out. I want to work on one set of edits before Cullen picks me up."

"And you call me a workaholic."

I snorted. "My producer got them to me late. It's okay, I'll get it done, but I feel bad. The author has a deadline."

"Then get it done, missy."

We hung up, and then I went to my small recording booth that I had put in a few years ago.

I was blessed to be able to be a voice actor and narrator. Though I had been doing it for a bit longer than Mercy had. In fact, I had been doing this full-time for ten years. I no longer needed to work as a drama teacher on the side or do tutoring for those who could afford it. And while I missed working with kids, the schools just didn't have the funding. And the year after I went full-time towards my dream, they cut the program entirely.

I still donated whatever time I had to private projects, and other pro bono work, so kids could have some form of creativity in their lives, but it wasn't enough.

However, I needed to seal myself into this booth and work on all the pickups that I might've missed.

For instance, instead of the word shallow, I had used the word sallow, which didn't really work for a shallow grave. I had also mixed up three words multiple times on a page, and I remembered that day I had been flustered for a reason I didn't want to think about.

Like how Cullen was coming over later that day to force me out of the house for dinner.

He was my friend. I needed to remember that. Just because he looked like Henry Cavill in his build, and most bearded of days, didn't mean that I needed to swoon over him.

It was just that now I knew he truly cared for his

beard. It was soft and smelled slightly of sandalwood soap and oil, meaning he had a true beard care routine that apparently did something for me. And when he wore Henleys, which he liked to do often, he would pull them up to his elbows, so he showed off his forearms. I didn't realize I had a fixation on those, but here I was, thinking about one of my friend's—one of my *best* friend's—forearms.

It was all I could do to remember that I had to be better than this. I wasn't going to ruin what we had. Because while I had my online community thanks to my job, Mercy and Cullen were really the only two people I saw on a regular basis. And even then, I tended to hermit more than anything. I enjoyed being a hermit. It was what I did.

But sometimes I needed to venture out. So I wasn't going to ruin one of the single connections I had to the outside world.

I was just going to have to get over this ridiculous crush when it came to Cullen.

It didn't take me long to get through my voice work, as I had been prepping for everything already, and as I sent the files to my editor, I quickly went back to my packing, ensuring that I had everything set up.

I looked down at the gift in silver wrapping

paper and wondered if it was too much. It wasn't like he was going to get me anything. We never had in the past. This would just be a thank you for driving me all the way to my parents' home in Wyoming gift.

Except that I had bought it for him weeks ago, but it wasn't as if I was going to show him the receipt.

Maybe he would think that I had left the house far too early in the morning, before the sun rose, and battled the stores for this.

Yes, that was how I was going to work it.

The doorbell rang as I closed my purse, the gift settled inside the large tote.

I swallowed hard and tried not to act as if I was a frantic lunatic.

This was just Cullen. I had been in a truck with him before.

Last night, in fact.

And it wasn't as if I had jumped him.

I quickly pushed those thoughts out of my mind and went to open the door.

And there he stood, in his lumberjack glory, and I knew this was going to be a problem.

He had on dark jeans that fit his thighs so well it should be illegal. He wore heavy work boots, but they were cleaner than his usual ones from the job site. Then he had a black flannel buttoned up over his Henley, and once again, his beard looked so soft.

I looked up into those blue eyes and let out a sigh.

I didn't realize that I had made an audible sigh until he narrowed his gaze at me.

"Good morning. You all packed?"

"Oh." I shook myself out of my reverie. Or fantasies. Whatever. "Yes. I'm all ready to go. Let me just grab everything."

"I'll help. You don't need to lift it into the back of the truck."

"I wasn't sure how much space you had, so I tried to stuff everything into my small suitcase."

"You didn't need to do that. I put the cover over the bed, and everything's padded in there. I have gifts for my siblings too, so thankfully playing Tetris is my pastime." He winked as he said it and lifted my over-packed suitcase as if it weighed nothing.

No, I wasn't going to stare at my best friend's muscles. I was just going to get over it and maybe drink some wine as soon as I got to my parents' home.

"All locked up?" he asked as I walked behind him, tote and purse in hand.

"Yes. Thank you for this by the way. Seriously."

"It's really no problem, Posy. Plus, you get to deal with my music. After all, I'm driving, I get control of the music."

"I'm not quite sure that's how it works," I said as I opened his passenger side door. I lifted one leg up onto the runners but slid forward as I hadn't realized that they were still icy.

"Whoa, I've got you." Cullen put his hands on my hips, keeping me steady, and I froze, blushing so hard I was afraid he could feel the intense heat radiating from me.

"Thank you. Icy, I guess." Yes, maybe if I used longer sentences, I wouldn't sound like such a dork.

"I have to lift into this truck, and I'm over six foot. But it helps with work." Then he proceeded to lift me into the cab of the truck with ease, setting me down softly onto the seat.

I just stared at him wide-eyed, wondering why I was reacting like this. I had known him for a long time now. Why was I acting as if I was just meeting this man for the first time?

But when his hands lingered for a second on my side before letting go, maybe this was a first.

I shook myself out of that once again, as he

closed the door behind him and moved around the front of the truck and hopped into his side.

"I forgot to ask if you wanted coffee or anything, so I got it anyway."

I grinned down at the familiar coffee cups from Latte on the Rocks, as well as the bag of pastries.

"I have my water bottle and a few snacks for the road." I dug into the tote and pulled out my container.

"A variety of cookies because I was bored, and then I have this too." I lifted another smaller container. "Tiny sandwiches that don't need to be in the cooler."

"How many Mary Poppins things are you going to pull out of that tote?" he asked as he turned on the engine.

I blushed, shaking my head. "You don't ask questions about a girl and her tote."

"With all my sisters you think I would've learned that already. Oh, you dropped this." He leaned forward, and I could feel his breath on my knee as he lifted the small silver-wrapped present.

"Oh, thank you." I chickened out as I grabbed the present from him and shoved it into the tote along with the containers.

"Anyway, I guess we should head out? I know you

texted the address to me and I put it into the GPS, but can you double check?"

I nodded, aware that we were both leaning towards each other, before I turned abruptly to the GPS and smiled.

"Looks right. Thank you for this again."

"If you don't stop thanking me, I'm going to open the window as we're driving through the snow and make you deal with it."

"You wouldn't."

He gave me a look that said he totally would, and frankly, with the way that I kept blushing and heating up, maybe snow in my face would help.

It was a good four-hour drive to my parents', which wasn't that far, however, I knew the roads weren't going to be easy. Cullen drove with ease, and I was grateful for his deep voice as he led the conversation. We spoke about silly things, work, the Montgomerys, and our favorite coffee place. It wasn't lost on me that he had gotten my order right. Even though I tended to switch between twenty different things, he had chosen the one that I drink most often.

I knew his coffee order as well, but it was easier since it was just a plain latte with skim milk and three sugars. But he had realized that I was in the mood for a winter latte during this season, complete with caramel, a dash of vanilla, and eggnog of all things. It sounded disgusting, but it was my true joy.

"Okay, I'm going to need one of those cookies."

I laughed as I bent over to dig into my bag for the container.

"Beware, I have six kinds."

"Where did you have time to make seven different kinds of cookies? Because I know it's not just one batch of each."

I shrugged as I opened the box so that I could show him what I had.

"I like baking. And I was able to give my neighbors cookies, as well as the local kids project that I worked with all semester.

"Those kids did a great job with their play. You did good, Posy."

I blushed, remembering seeing him in the back row, cheering for the director, rather than the kids.

Because he had shown up as my friend, just as Mercy had, and I needed to remember that.

Friend.

"I have sugar cookies, frosted sugar cookies, chocolate chip, oatmeal chocolate chip because raisins do not belong in cookies, peanut butter kisses, peanut butter sugar cookies, and strawberry shortcake kisses."

"I have no idea what two of those are, but a kiss? I'll take one of those."

His face drained of color for a moment, before he cleared his throat and focused on the road.

"I meant the strawberry one. That sounds good."

"No problem. However, I just realized I forgot napkins."

"Open the glove box, I have a whole set there."

I did so, noting the emergency kit, the glass breaker thing, and wet wipes. He did seem to have everything.

I handed him two cookies over a napkin and flinched as our fingers touched. He nearly dropped the cookies, but kept his gaze on the road so he didn't swerve.

"Sorry, fumbling today."

"It's no problem, Posy." He took a bite and groaned. The type of groan that made me think of things I shouldn't.

"Dear God, Posy. How have I not had more of your baked goods?"

"Well, I'm apparently greedy when it comes to hoarding my goods."

I blinked, wondering how that sounded somewhat sexual even though it wasn't at all, but from the way that the tips of Cullen's ears pinked, maybe I wasn't the only one feeling awkward after last night.

"So Cullen, about…" My voice trailed off.

"Yeah. I wanted to apologize."

My gaze shot to his even though he kept his on the road. The snow was starting to pile up, and I knew it was getting harder for him to drive. However, we hadn't been skidding, and he was going slow enough that he seemed safe. So I was going to trust him. Because he was Cullen.

"Apologize," I finally said, my mind catching up with his words.

"I didn't mean to put you on the spot like that."

"You didn't. The Montgomerys did. And, well, I didn't mind it. It's a kiss. Right?" I asked, feeling awkward as hell.

"Yeah. A kiss. And I guess it was better than me kissing Lex or something," he said dryly.

I rolled my eyes, and turned my attention to forward, and blinked.

"The flakes are getting heavier."

"I know," he said through gritted teeth.

That's when I realized that both his hands were on the steering wheel, his knuckles white. "Do we need to pull over?" I asked, fear sliding up my spine.

"Can you check your phone for the weather and see if we can get any service for the weather app? Because this seems more like a squall than it should be. We weren't supposed to get snow like this in any area of either state until tomorrow morning. I wouldn't have driven us this way if I had known."

I pulled up my app and cursed. "The entire section is white and blue. They're saying that it developed far earlier than they were planning. Why didn't we get any alerts?"

He shook his head. "I guess service worked for some, but not for everyone. Fuck. Okay, we're going to keep going because I do not want to be stuck on the side of the road. We do have enough gas, but it's not safe."

I nodded, my hand on the center console handle, putting more trust in Cullen than any other person I knew.

"We've got this Posy, okay?"

"I know. I trust you."

I watched his throat work as he swallowed hard, and then we both sat in silence, the radio off as we made our way through the now darkening roads. It was still the middle of the day, and yet it didn't feel like it at all.

"There's a set of cabins with vacancy less than a mile away. I think we need to stop."

I tensed, nerves racking me for more than one reason. "Just to get through the storm. I don't know if I really want to be on the roads much longer."

"Exactly. Just hold on."

Headlights flashed in the distance, and Cullen cursed, and I couldn't help but hold on tight as everything shifted in an instant. The headlights seemed to brighten as the glared in our eyes before they turned slightly crooked.

Cullen turned the steering wheel, his shoulders tense, but then it was too late. The car in front of us swerved to the side and hit the embankment, as the car coming towards us, headlights spinning, but we were still too close. It didn't clip us, but we spun, the ice beneath the wheels too much. I blinked as headlights shone, and then there was darkness, then headlights again as we did a circle and a half, before a roaring sound filled my ears, and we slammed into the icy side of the road.

And finally, the scream that I had been holding, escaped.

# CHAPTER 3

## CULLEN

Heart pounding, I thankfully was able to right the truck, the embankment not too far away from the road, but I put the truck in park and turned towards Posy. "Are you okay? Are you hurt? Talk to me."

It tasted like metal on my tongue, just thinking about what could have happened. None of the other cars had stopped. In fact, the one that had spun out had kept going. The other cars that passed us probably couldn't even see us in this near whiteout. My lights were on, so maybe they thought we were just parked on the side of the road, but I didn't know. I didn't have time to think about some asshat who had been driving too fast on icy roads, when we all should have been tucked safe at home anyway.

"I'm fine. No bumps or bruises, you weren't going that fast, and you leaned into the skid like you were supposed to. That's right, right? Leaning into the skid? I clearly don't remember driver's ed. And thank God I wasn't in my car."

That metallic taste turned to bile at the thought of her in that crappy sedan trying to make it through this snowstorm. "Well, we don't have to think about that, because your car's safe back at the Montgomerys'."

"I'm going to have to deal with that soon."

"You know they said that it was easier just to keep it there than take it to a place when it's most likely closed anyway. So come on. Let's figure out what the hell we're going to do."

I still wanted to run my hands over her, to check to make sure she was safe, but I resisted. Barely.

"Do you think we can get out of this ditch?" she asked, her voice shaky.

"I hope to hell we can. Thankfully I don't think it's too big of a ditch. And there were those cabins not too far. I don't want to have to walk in this."

She shuddered. "No. Let's not."

Praying to whatever gods were listening, I pulled back onto the road, grateful there were no cars in the way.

It only took a few minutes of white-knuckle driving, and me doing my best not to look over to ensure that Posy was safe, for us to find the entrance to the cabins. There was a vacancy sign, though I didn't know how many others had pulled off. There were already a few cars with their lights on, telling me they had just pulled in as well.

"You stay here, and I'll go check to see if they have a place to stay. At least for a little bit."

"You don't have to keep the truck on, let's save gas."

"If you get even a little bit cold, you turn the truck on. Got me?"

"Yes, Daddy."

Even as she said the words, her mouth pressed into a thin line, and we just met each other's gazes. I was not going to think about that or go down any path that was going to be too much. As it was, I had a feeling if we were lucky, we were going to be spending the night alone together in a cabin. If we were unlucky, we'd be alone in my truck.

Fuck.

I opened the door, braving it against the strong wind as that shock of cold air hit my face.

With gritted teeth, I jumped out of the truck and

slammed the door closed, hopefully keeping as much of the warm air in there as possible.

The snow was already starting to pile up, and I trudged my way down what I hoped was a path towards the front office. I stomped the snow off my shoes and opened up the door, hoping to hell we were going to have options.

There were a few snowbound people in the room, and an older couple behind the desk. They each had worried expressions on their faces, tight brows, pinched mouths, but when they looked at the person in front of them, they gave a sad smile, and yet, kept handing out keys.

"Okay, your cabin's out the back, you're going to have to trudge through some more snow, my son's out there helping out another couple with their luggage, and he'll be there to help you."

An older gentleman shook his head. "You keep him warm. I've got it. I'm just grateful you have this."

"We have ways of getting to you, and we like snow. And don't worry, we also have food coming to you. We're not going to let anybody starve in this storm."

I was pretty sure we had just found an oasis, and I had to hope there was space for us.

I moved up to the counter, rolling my shoulders back as I prayed. "Should I ask if you have a room at the inn?" I asked, trying to keep my tone light.

The older woman smiled softly. "We do. All of the cabins were booked, however, not a single one can make it for the next two days thanks to this storm that popped up far too quickly. So we have ways to make this work. We're running out though, so I can only give you one, is that okay?"

Thinking of being alone in a room with Posy was going to be a little too much, but I would deal with that later. I would keep her warm and safe, and that was all that mattered.

"That's just fine. Thank you."

"And we're not jacking up the rates, this was the normal rate. You can look it up online."

"You guys are a godsend."

"No, we've just been in your shoes." She looked over at her husband who was helping a family of five with three small children move towards the edge of the lodge.

"There are a few rooms inside this main building, but we thought we would keep those for any families. I hope that's okay."

"Keep the kids safe and warm. We should be good out there."

"You have a mini generator, as well as everything you would need in a cabin. We'll send out food, and there should be a welcome basket in the room. Here are your keys and checkout is when the storm ends," she said with a laugh. "We'll call the cabin through the landline, and through your cell phone that you provided just in case. We're going to get through this. It's the Colorado and Wyoming border, it's what we do."

"You're right about that," I said as I zipped up my jacket once more and braved the snow to get to the truck.

The truck that was still not on.

Growling, I stomped my way towards my vehicle and opened the door.

"I thought you were going to turn on the truck when you were cold," I snapped.

Posy sat with her knees up to her chest on her seat, a blanket that she must have pulled out of her tote around her shoulders.

"I can't see my breath yet, so I wasn't sure if we needed to save gas."

"I'm going to leave my truck here, but we only have to head over towards the cabin in the back."

Her eyes widened, a smile filling her face. "They had room for us?"

"I'm pretty sure we've found the nicest couple in this area. Ever. So yes, they not only have a spot for us, but we're about to get food."

"I think I love them."

"It's okay, we can propose marriage to them later, let's get inside, and I'll get all the luggage."

"You don't have to do that, I can help."

"Carry what you can. The snow's died down for a little bit, but I know another gust is coming."

It only took one trip considering we had left some of the gifts in my triple-locked truck. If somebody wanted to get in there to steal things, we were going to have way more problems than that. But we had a clean set of clothes, toiletries, and that magical tote.

By the time we set everything down, took off our jackets, and warmed up by the actual fireplace, the awkwardness settled in.

I was about to spend the night in a room with one of my best friends, doing my best not to think about it.

Just because I constantly wanted to touch her, to taste her, didn't mean I was going to let myself do that.

"Oh, that's my folks," Posy said with a small smile.

"I texted them and said I was going to be late, so here's the call."

"Damn it, I should text my folks. You go to the other side of the cabin, and I'll try to let you have some privacy."

She blushed and answered.

"Hi Mom. Dad."

As I texted my folks letting them know that we were safe, exactly where we were, and that we wouldn't be there until tomorrow at the earliest, I did my best not to listen to Posy's conversation. However, it was sort of hard to do. While the cabin was recently stocked and decorated, it still was not that big.

"I'm perfectly safe. You know Cullen."

"We do, and we're glad that he's able to take care of you, but we worry. You're all alone. And you're alone so often. And I know you say that you can handle that, but we worry about our baby girl."

I winced at that, knowing she probably hated the phrase.

"Mom. I'm fine. And I can take care of myself."

"Oh yes, you're an independent woman. And we love that for you."

I winced at the tone, but Posy just let out a breath..

"Yes, I know. I am woman hear me roar. However, that's not going to be an issue tonight. All I have to do is make sure that the generator works, and we have food in our bellies. Cullen's truck can get through most storms, just not this one."

"Okay baby. Just text and let us know how you're doing throughout the night."

"Mom. I'm thirty-five."

"We know. But we worry."

I sighed. "You didn't text like this when David and I were married."

"Because he was there to protect you. To take care of you."

Posy met my gaze and rolled her eyes. "Well Cullen's here to protect me for the night. So you don't have to worry, okay?"

"Oh you're right. That's good."

I pressed my lips together at the annoyed look on her face, before she crossed her eyes as she tilted the phone away so they couldn't see her face.

"Anyway, I love you and I'll see you soon. Merry Christmas."

"Merry Christmas baby girl."

When she ended the call, she growled at her phone. "Thirty-five. I'm thirty-five years old."

"Well, I'm thirty-nine. We can both be old and yet beholden to our parents."

"I bet your parents knew that you were going to be safe."

"My mom did ask for me to check-in as often as possible," I said dryly.

"Because she's worried about an ax murderer or a storm, not because you can't take care of yourself."

I winced. "Yeah, what is up with that?"

"I'm going to need a lot more vodka in order to have that conversation."

I snapped my fingers and grinned.

"Well, not only do I know that there's a bottle of wine in that welcome basket, I have something special."

I rooted around in my suitcase and pulled out a bottle of vodka. "I can go stick it in the snow, and make sure it's nice and icy for us."

"You have vodka?"

"Because my parents don't drink, and while they totally allow their kids to drink, we have to bring our own."

"So I'm taking away your family Christmas vodka?"

"I have another bottle. Mostly because there are nine of us, plus spouses. It adds up."

"You're a lifesaver. Once again. I don't know what I'd do without you," she sing-songed.

"You're just going to have to show how appreciative you are later."

We both paused, and I realized how sexual that sounded, but as the room began to warm, I realized I really didn't care.

"Okay, let's get prepared for a long night. Hopefully we can leave as soon as the storm's up."

"And they plow the roads," I mumbled.

She winced, but didn't say anything, but she did go straight for the wine.

A few hours later, we were glad that we also had enough water to drown out the amount of alcohol in our systems. The box lunches had been fantastic, as well as the cheese board that could nearly rival a decent basic Montgomery charcuterie board.

"It wasn't that David and I hated each other, it was that we didn't like each other in the end."

"So that's why you two got divorced? You just didn't like each other?"

"No, we got divorced because he liked our neighbor's vagina more than mine."

I coughed on my vodka soda and set down my glass.

"Are you fucking kidding me?"

"Nope. I thought we were doing just fine, trying for children, and when that didn't work out, he tried with others. Go me."

"Do you need me to kill him? I mean if I can't, I have siblings. And I know the Montgomerys would help."

Her lips twitched. "Oddly you just saying that helps. But don't worry. He's already divorced from her, and working on his third wife. Still no children, but it turns out he didn't want any."

I winced. "I'm sorry."

"I'm really over it. He's an asshole, but he's not part of my life. Much to the chagrin of my parents."

"Did they like him?"

"They loved him. And they loved that I wasn't alone."

"I'm sorry."

"I don't think they realize that there's a difference between being alone and being lonely. Yes, I tend to hermit, but that's because I work from home. I like being comfortable. And I go out with people some-times." She paused as my lips twitched. "Okay I go out with you. To the point that my neighbor thought we were dating."

I blinked. "Oh?"

"Yes, because you constantly pick me up, so we don't have to drive my beater of a car."

"You can afford a better car."

"I know. I'm just cheap. And I like that car. I bought it with my own money that I made from narrating books. Not from anything having to do with David."

"That's good then."

"I think so. And it's sad to say goodbye, but it's time. However, I'm not lonely. And technically I'm not alone. You're here."

"How much have you had to drink if you're already thinking about that," I asked softly.

"Not enough," she mumbled. "What about you. I know you were married."

I shrugged, looking down at my nearly empty glass. "Nothing too exciting. We got married young, and I thought we liked each other, and then we didn't. I don't think she liked that I'm a blue-collar worker. She wanted to travel, to see the world, and do it while in suites, rather than on a budget."

"Are you kidding me? Having someone that knows how to take care of a house is one of the main things I'm looking for in a man."

"Oh really?" I asked with a laugh.

"Yes. Because I hate home maintenance."

"So you would just marry someone for what, the size of their hammer? Not their bank account?"

Our gazes met and we burst out laughing.

And when I leaned forward, that's when I realized that both of us were practically knee-to-knee on the couch. The warmth of her seeped into my body, and I swallowed hard.

My breath quickened, our noses practically brushing, and when her tongue darted out to lick her lips, I was lost.

"Tell me no. Just tell me no."

"I don't want to tell you no."

And then my mouth was on hers. Somehow, we set down the glasses, and I cupped her face, needing her taste.

This wasn't like last time, not a quick graze of lips and then jumping away from each other. This was hot and needy, and all I wanted to do was explore her mouth, and then the rest of her. Her hands went around my body, sliding up my shirt so her nails dug into my skin, and I moaned into her.

"That's it, dig in," I growled.

"Please tell me you brought a condom."

I blinked and grinned. "Just call me a Boy Scout. Always prepared."

She snorted but then pressed her lips against mine once again.

We spent far too long and yet not enough kissing, exploring each other, learning each other's tastes.

And when my cock threatened to burst out of my jeans, I lifted her up by the waist and carried her the short distance to the bed.

She let out a gasp, and I kept moving, tugging on her jeans.

"You're going to have to work on your shirt, because I don't think I can wait that long."

"Impatient. I like it."

And then we were moving quickly, and her jeans were off in one corner, her panties in another. I tore off my shirt, shoved down my pants, and then both of us were finally naked, and I went to my knees.

I pulled her to the edge of the bed, grabbing her by her hips before I wrapped my arms around her thighs, and finally had my first taste.

"Cullen!"

"You taste like fucking honey," I growled against her pussy before I took another taste, and then another. I licked at her clit before sliding one finger in between her soft folds.

"You're swollen for me. Look how wet you are. Is this all for me?"

She went up to her elbows and looked down between us, not a shy glance in sight.

"Of course you do that to me, Cullen. Just like I know that erection that looks so painful is for me."

"Damn straight."

There was a difference between having sex in your twenties and then when you were nearly forty. Because you knew what you were doing. You could take your time, slowly figure out exactly what the other person needed, craved.

I lapped at her cunt, loving the way she practically shot off the bed as I found her g-spot, and curled my fingers, knowing she was finally going to come. When she arched off the bed, her hands on her breasts and her pussy clamping around my fingers, I just grinned. Then I licked her off my lips and reached in my bag for a condom.

It wasn't as if I had known this would happen, but a man always likes to be prepared.

I tore the foil and slid the condom down my length as she watched, her gaze wide.

"Posy, I can stop."

"If you don't get inside me right now, I'm going to first, make myself come, and then scream."

"Okay, understood."

And then I stood up, took her by the hips, and shoved into her with one thrust.

We both froze, her cunt taut, tight, and all mine, and I swallowed hard.

"I'm going to have to start playing football stats or something, because I cannot come in two strokes."

"I think you can handle more." And then she reached up for me, so I lowered down, taking her mouth.

I slid out slowly, inch by inch, before I rocked my way back inside her.

She met me thrust for thrust, both of us taking in one another with each gasp. When I moved, shifting so I was on my back and she was finally riding me, I had my hands on her breasts, pinching at her nipples as she threw her head back and rode me like Goddess Divine.

I moved one hand down, flicking my thumb over her clit, and when she came, I grit my teeth, telling myself I could not come yet.

No, I needed to let her come one more time.

Dazed, I pulled her into my arms, so we lay on our sides, her breasts to my front, and I slid back into her, lifting her leg up over my hips.

And with that, so close I could feel every breath,

every touch, I rocked in and out of her, slowly at first, and then harder, faster, until we were both panting each other's names. And finally, *finally* she came once more, and I followed, moaning her name and taking her mouth as everything happened, and then went blurry.

Because this was the perfect moment in time.

And I had to hope it wasn't the last.

# CHAPTER 4

## POSY

The morning came far too quickly, the sun dancing over my eyelids. I did my best not to shift, not to make a single move. Because if I did, he would know I was awake.

His body rolled over me, protectively holding me in his embrace as if we had been doing this for decades rather than the few short hours we had given each other to sleep.

I wanted to say that I could blame it all on the alcohol, but that wasn't going to be the case. It couldn't be when I had been clear in my intentions, my consent, and the fact that the only regret I had was that it was going to be the last time.

My head didn't ache, which told me indeed I hadn't had too much to drink, and I was grateful for the water we had chugged in between our bouts of heat.

Though heat wasn't the right word for it.

Glimpses of exactly what had happened the night before filled my brain, and I let out a sigh without thinking.

Because he had made sure that everything we had done was exactly how I had always thought it would be.

Rough and yet soft, caring and attentive, and yet giving each other pleasure in a way that I hadn't thought possible before. I ached between my legs, and I knew I would be sore for a couple of days. My breasts were tender, and I knew tiny little bite marks and bruises would cover my body, and it would all be taken in pleasure, and memory. Just like I knew he had similar marks over him.

One set of sheets was tangled on the floor—we had found a spare in the closet—and now we were huddled under layers of blankets and quilts, with his front to my back, his leg positioned perfectly between mine so that we spooned into one another. I could feel his rock-hard erection pressing against my lower back, but neither one of us shifted.

Because Cullen had heard that sigh of mine. His arm tightened around my waist, and that's when I realized his large hand cupped my breast, as if he had done it in his sleep, a perfect space to nestle after a long day.

My lips curved at that thought, and I had to wonder exactly what he would think about that.

"I know you're awake," he whispered. His warm breath slid over the back of my neck, and I shivered into his hold, unconsciously snuggling in for more warmth.

Truly we hadn't needed the countless quilts and blankets. Not when he was a heater himself.

"Posy? Would you like me to get out of bed?" he asked softly, and I swallowed hard before turning in his hold.

He shifted slightly, and now his cock pressed against my belly, our legs entangled. I put my hands on his chest, nearly covering my breasts as I looked up at him.

"I'm awake."

"Yes. You are," he repeated.

Of course I hadn't said the correct thing. After all, I felt beyond lost. Beyond trying to figure out what the heck I was doing.

"I can see the panic in your eyes," he said after a moment, and I bit into my lip, my hands curling against his chest.

When he let out a deep sigh, I scrambled out of bed, not knowing what I should do.

If I reached for him, I wouldn't be able to stop. I wasn't sure what he would do though. And that was the worst of it all.

Because he was my friend. And now I was afraid I was going to lose him.

"Posy," he said after a moment. He sat up, the blankets pulling around his waist. When he slid his hands through his hair, pushing it back from his face, I pressed my lips together. I'd wrapped one of the quilts around myself, standing there as if I were lost beyond redemption.

"I'm… I don't know what to say."

"I guess you don't have to say anything." He frowned, and I shook my head, feeling as if I were losing something precious. "Did I hurt you?"

My gaze shot up, meeting his, and I moved forward without thinking. He stood up quickly, tying one of the sheets around his waist, and I put my hands against his chest once more.

"You didn't hurt me at all, anything that happened was exactly what either one of us wanted. At least at the time…" I said, my voice trailing off. Cullen cursed and pulled away from me. It was as if ice slowly began to make its jagged way through my chest, and one of the only people I could ever rely on walked away, leaving me a broken husk.

"I'm sorry. I really shouldn't have kissed you. Either time. I mean, I don't want to ruin what we have. You're one of my best friends. I love hanging out with you, I just like being with you. But I don't know. I mean, you're one of the only people who helps me get out of my house. How silly is that? And here we are, ruining it because we can't help what our glands want. And I just said the word glands. Who says the word glands?" I asked, my voice rising with each panicked sentence.

Cullen was in front of me then and cupped my face.

"I'm going to need you to breathe, baby. Breathe."

"Did you call me baby?" I asked, my voice slightly breathy.

When his lips curved, I smiled at him. "Yes, I did call you baby. Though I'm going to need to find another cute name for you. Too many of our friends use the word baby."

"Oh."

"I need you to calm down, okay? Because I think we need to talk."

"Usually it's the woman saying that."

"In movies from the nineties and aughts, but not

now. We're going to move forward, because, Posy, I've been falling in love with you. There." He lowered his hands and began to pace again as I stood there, barely keeping the quilt over my shoulders.

Had he just said what I thought he did? No, there was no way. Cullen could not love me. Or at least start to fall in love with me. We hadn't even kissed before the mistletoe. And yet…

"Love?" I croaked.

He winced before reaching for his jeans.

"I can't have this conversation when we're both naked."

"Oh, thank God. Because I'm one panicked movement away from losing this quilt, and then it's one of my worst nightmares. Having an awkward conversation with someone you care about and then you're both naked."

He winced when I said the word care, and I knew I needed to fix it. I just didn't know how. I really wasn't good at this.

"Here, we sort of piled your clothes last night. And well, we do have our suitcases for clean ones."

I nodded, then pulled on my jeans and a sweater. I'd shower and change for real later, but I didn't have time to make an outfit when my life seemed to be changing with each passing gasp.

"You said love."

"I did. And I've been freaking out about it for a while now."

"Why didn't you ever say anything?"

"Probably because I was afraid I was going to fuck it up. Much like I'm doing right now. Yes, Posy. I'm falling in love with you."

"But you never said anything."

"Yes. I realize that." That's when I realized we were just repeating the same circular argument, and I let out a breath.

"I didn't know. I just thought we were friends."

"We are friends, Posy. You are one of my favorite people in the world and I wasn't going to ruin our friendship, ruin what we already have together for what could have just been our glands, as you put it."

"We must never use that word again."

"I agree," he said, his lips twitching. "But in all seriousness, I didn't know what you felt. I still don't know what you feel. So I wasn't about to ruin a great thing in my life. I'm almost forty, Posy. I'm not a fucking kid. I've had serious relationships. Fuck, I've been married. Just like you."

I nodded, trying not to think about my ex-husband in that moment.

"We've been through this before with other

people. And we both know what happens when it doesn't work out. It's shitty, and then you lose that person in your life. But I wasn't friends with my ex-wife before we got married. And things didn't work out for either one of us. But I don't know what I'm going to do if I lose you now. My family is huge. There's so many of us, and they're all starting families now. I'm one of the only ones left unmarried, and I was the first one to even cross that bridge. And here I am, standing in front of you, feeling like a goddamn teenager because I don't know how to tell you that I want to be in your life. I don't want this to be a one-night mistake."

"Cullen," I interjected.

"It's okay, I'll get you to your parents' house, and we can forget this ever happened."

"Cullen. Please listen to me. Because now you're the one freaking out."

"I guess I am, aren't I?" he asked, that grin on his face again.

"I'm thirty-five. I've been married before, and I know that according to society I'm too late or nearly too late to begin a family, but I want one. It wasn't in the cards the first time, and frankly, I'm not sure if it'll ever happen, but you as my friend? I want that to always be."

"Damn straight."

"And I want a chance to fall in love with you, Cullen," I said, eyes widened. "I want a chance to figure out something that could be amazing. And take a leap that I was so afraid to do. I've lost too many years, and I don't want to lose anymore."

And then Cullen was in front of me, hands on my cheeks again. "Thirties aren't the end you know, at least that's what my friends tell me."

"That is true, but maybe they can be a new beginning?"

"Look at you, sounding like one of those books you narrate."

"I want a chance to fall in love with you Cullen," I repeated.

"Good. Then you can catch up."

And then his mouth was on mine, and I knew that being snowed in with my best friend might have been the best near accident ever.

*FIVE YEARS LATER.*

. . .

"TASHA, PLEASE STOP BANGING THAT SPOON AGAINST that pan," I said as sweetly as I could as my three-year-old daughter sat on the floor, grinning up at me.

"Yes, I know you love that pan, but Mommy has a headache."

"Mom! Mom!" Jake said as he ran into the room, our eight-year-old son grinning at us with his backpack over his shoulder. Cullen walked in behind him, our infant daughter in his arms.

"Oh, did you get your paper back?" I asked, smiling as Jake wrapped his arms around my waist.

"I got an A. Can you believe that? Me."

"I'm not surprised at all," I said with a grin.

In the past five years, life wasn't always easy, but I had learned to take a second chance when I never thought it was possible.

Because not only on that long stretch of road did I fall in love with my best friend, I also started a whole new life I was never prepared for.

Because we not only celebrated Christmas at my parents' house, we celebrated the day after Christmas with all of Cullen's family.

Because just like that, we were family.

After all, we had been accidentally dating for a

good two years. Just nobody ever bothered to tell us we were already on that path.

We had adopted Tasha and Jake together, only a little over two years ago now, and they were two joys and lights in our lives. So having baby Natalie at the ripe age of forty, had been quite a shock. We hadn't been trying, because neither one of us had wanted to worry ourselves like we had the first two years, and now, here we were, proud parents of three, and exhausted.

I spun Jake around the room, before picking up Tasha and watching as Cullen walked towards me, Natalie still in his arms, looking happily up at her father.

"I thought you were going to take a nap," Cullen whispered before sliding his lips over mine. I sighed into him, that familiar feel of him still feeling new at the same time. The paradox of it unyielding.

"I was in the mood for a snack, and you had kidnapped my baby girl."

"She needed Daddy time, and now Jake's home from school, and I see Tasha is starting a band," he said as he tickled our daughter.

I sat Tasha down, and she chased after Jake, before Cullen handed me Natalie and forced me to sit down on one of the kitchen chairs.

Then I proceeded to watch the love of my life make us dinner, cleaning up messes and letting me rest.

Because this was the man who had not only gotten me out of my house all those years ago but had broken me out of my shell.

And I loved him more than anything.

"Hey, did you hear our favorite cabin is open for the next holiday season."

"You do realize that both sets of our parents will murder us if we spend Christmas in a cabin alone."

"That is true, but I already have a plan."

"Oh?" I asked, keeping an eye on the two other kids while I nursed Natalie.

"We're heading to my folks' house, and your parents will be there as well, then we're going to have Mommy and Daddy time only thirty minutes away in our favorite cabin."

"Are you telling me that you want me to leave a then six-month-old, as well as the other two, with both sets of grandparents?" He opened his mouth, probably to explain what a good idea it was, but I started laughing. "I'm in. Totally in."

He moved around the kitchen island and pressed his lips against mine again. "That's good, because I already booked it. I'm evil that way."

"I guess it's good that one of us takes the initiative."

"With you, I'll do anything."

And then he went back to cooking dinner, and I nestled in my chair, forever grateful for a snowstorm, a broken car, and a tiny cabin in the woods.

**If you'd like to read the next Generation with the Montgomery Ink Legacy Series: Bittersweet Promises**

**In the mood to read another family saga? Meet the Cage Family in The Forever Rule!**

**In the mood for more small town romance? Check out the Ashford Creek series with LEGACY. Or as I like to call it "The Small Town of Single Dads".**

# ALSO FROM CARRIE ANN RYAN

**The Montgomery Ink Legacy Series:**
Book 1: Bittersweet Promises (Leif & Brooke)
Book 2: At First Meet (Nick & Lake)
Book 2.5: Happily Ever Never (May & Leo)
Book 3: Longtime Crush (Sebastian & Raven)
Book 4: Best Friend Temptation (Noah, Ford, and Greer)
Book 4.5: Happily Ever Maybe (Jennifer & Gus)
Book 5: Last First Kiss (Daisy & Hugh)
Book 6: His Second Chance (Kane & Phoebe)
Book 7: One Night with You (Kingston & Claire)
Book 8: Accidentally Forever (Crew & Aria)
Book 9: Last Chance Seduction (Lexington & Mercy)
Book 10: Kiss Me Forever (Brooklyn & Reece)

Book 11: His Guilty Pleasure (Dash & Aly)

Book 12: Maybe it's You (Riley & Gage)

**The Cage Family**

Book 1: The Forever Rule (Aston & Blakely)

Book 2: An Unexpected Everything (Isabella & Weston)

Book 3: If You Were Mine (Dorian & Harper)

Book 4: One Quick Obsession (Hudson & Scarlett)

Book 5: Pretend it's Forever (Sophia & Carson)

Book 6: Wish it Were You (Flynn & Luna)

**Ashford Creek**

Book 1: Legacy (Callum & Felicity)

Book 2: Crossroads (Bodhi & Kiera)

Book 3: Westward (Atlas & Elizabeth)

Book 4: Patience (Teagan & Rush)

**Clover Lake**

Book 1: Always a Fake Bridesmaid (Livvy & Ewan)

Book 2: Accidental Runaway Groom (Jamie & Sharp)

Book 3: His Practically Fake Proposal (Galen & Addy)

**The Wilder Brothers Series:**

Book 1: One Way Back to Me (Eli & Alexis)

Book 2: Always the One for Me (Evan & Kendall)

Book 3: The Path to You (Everett & Bethany)

Book 4: Coming Home for Us (Elijah & Maddie)

Book 5: Stay Here With Me (East & Lark)

Book 6: Finding the Road to Us (Elliot, Trace, and Sidney)

Book 7: Moments for You (Ridge & Aurora)

Book 7.5: A Wilder Wedding (Amos & Naomi)

Book 8: Forever For Us (Wyatt & Ava)

Book 9: Pieces of Me (Gabriel & Briar)

Book 10: Endlessly Yours (Brooks & Rory)

**The Falling for the Cassidy Brothers Series:**

*(Formerly the First Time Series)*

Book 1: Good Time Boyfriend (Heath & Devney)

Book 2: Last Minute Fiancé (Luca & Addison)

Book 3: Second Chance Husband (August & Paisley)

**Montgomery Ink Denver:**

Book 0.5: <u>Ink Inspired </u>(Shep & Shea)

Book 0.6: <u>Ink Reunited </u>(Sassy, Rare, and Ian)

Book 1: <u>Delicate Ink </u>(Austin & Sierra)

Book 1.5: <u>Forever Ink </u>(Callie & Morgan)

Book 2: <u>Tempting Boundaries </u>(Decker and Miranda)

Book 3: <u>Harder than Words </u>(Meghan & Luc)

Book 3.5: <u>Finally Found You </u>(Mason & Presley)

Book 4: <u>Written in Ink </u>(Griffin & Autumn)

Book 4.5: <u>Hidden Ink </u>(Hailey & Sloane)

Book 5: <u>Ink Enduring </u>(Maya, Jake, and Border)

Book 6: <u>Ink Exposed </u>(Alex & Tabby)

Book 6.5: <u>Adoring Ink </u>(Holly & Brody)

Book 6.6: <u>Love, Honor, & Ink </u>(Arianna & Harper)

Book 7: <u>Inked Expressions </u>(Storm & Everly)

Book 7.3: <u>Dropout </u>(Grayson & Kate)

Book 7.5: <u>Executive Ink </u>(Jax & Ashlynn)

Book 8: <u>Inked Memories </u>(Wes & Jillian)

Book 8.5: <u>Inked Nights </u>(Derek & Olivia)

Book 8.7: <u>Second Chance Ink </u>(Brandon & Lauren)

Book 8.5: Montgomery Midnight Kisses (Alex & Tabby Bonus(

Bonus: Inked Kingdom (Stone & Sarina)


**Montgomery Ink: Colorado Springs**

Book 1: Fallen Ink (Adrienne & Mace)

Book 2: Restless Ink (Thea & Dimitri)

Book 2.5: Ashes to Ink (Abby & Ryan)

Book 3: Jagged Ink (Roxie & Carter)

Book 3.5: Ink by Numbers (Landon & Kaylee)

**The Montgomery Ink: Boulder Series:**

Book 1: Wrapped in Ink (Liam & Arden)

Book 2: Sated in Ink (Ethan, Lincoln, and Holland)

Book 3: Embraced in Ink (Bristol & Marcus)

Book 3: Moments in Ink (Zia & Meredith)

Book 4: Seduced in Ink (Aaron & Madison)

Book 4.5: Captured in Ink (Julia, Ronin, & Kincaid)

Book 4.7: Inked Fantasy (Secret ??)

Book 4.8: A Very Montgomery Christmas (The Entire Boulder Family)

**The Montgomery Ink: Fort Collins Series:**

Book 1: Inked Persuasion (Jacob & Annabelle)

Book 2: Inked Obsession (Beckett & Eliza)

Book 3: Inked Devotion (Benjamin & Brenna)

Book 3.5: Nothing But Ink (Clay & Riggs)

Book 4: Inked Craving (Lee & Paige)

Book 5: Inked Temptation (Archer & Killian)

**The Promise Me Series:**

Book 1: Forever Only Once (Cross & Hazel)

Book 2: From That Moment (Prior & Paris)

Book 3: Far From Destined (Macon & Dakota)

Book 4: From Our First (Nate & Myra)

**The Whiskey and Lies Series:**

Book 1: <u>Whiskey Secrets</u> (Dare & Kenzie)

Book 2: <u>Whiskey Reveals</u> (Fox & Melody)

Book 3: <u>Whiskey Undone</u> (Loch & Ainsley)

**The Gallagher Brothers Series:**

Book 1: <u>Love Restored</u> (Graham & Blake)

Book 2: <u>Passion Restored</u> (Owen & Liz)

Book 3: <u>Hope Restored</u> (Murphy & Tessa)

**The Carr Family Series:**

*(Formerly the Less Than Series)*

Book 1: Breathless With Her (Devin & Erin)

Book 2: Reckless With You (Tucker & Amelia)

Book 3: Shameless With Him (Caleb & Zoey)

**The Fractured Connections Series:**

Book 1: Breaking Without You (Cameron & Violet)

Book 2: Shouldn't Have You (Brendon & Harmony)

Book 3: Falling With You (Aiden & Sienna)

Book 4: Taken With You (Beckham & Meadow)

**The Campus Roommates Series:**

*(Formerly the On My Own Series)*

Book 0.5: My First Glance

Book 1: My One Night (Dillon & Elise)

Book 2: My Rebound (Pacey & Mackenzie)

Book 3: My Next Play (Miles & Nessa)

Book 4: My Bad Decisions (Tanner & Natalie)

**The Ravenwood Coven Series:**

Book 1: Dawn Unearthed

Book 2: Dusk Unveiled

Book 3: Evernight Unleashed

**The Aspen Pack Series:**

Book 1: Etched in Honor

Book 2: Hunted in Darkness

Book 3: Mated in Chaos

Book 4: Harbored in Silence

Book 5: Marked in Flames

**The Talon Pack:**

Book 1: Tattered Loyalties

Book 2: An Alpha's Choice

Book 3: Mated in Mist

Book 4: Wolf Betrayed

Book 5: Fractured Silence

Book 6: <u>Destiny Disgraced</u>

Book 7: <u>Eternal Mourning</u>

Book 8: <u>Strength Enduring</u>

Book 9: <u>Forever Broken</u>

Book 10: Mated in Darkness

Book 11: Fated in Winter

**Redwood Pack Series:**

Book 0.5: <u>An Alpha's Path</u>

Book 1: <u>A Taste for a Mate</u>

Book 2: <u>Trinity Bound</u>

Book 2.5: <u>A Night Away</u>

Book 3: <u>Enforcer's Redemption</u>

Book 3.5: <u>Blurred Expectations</u>

Book 3.7: <u>Forgiveness</u>

Book 4: <u>Shattered Emotions</u>

Book 5: <u>Hidden Destiny</u>

Book 5.5: <u>A Beta's Haven</u>

Book 6: <u>Fighting Fate</u>

Book 6.5: <u>Loving the Omega</u>

Book 6.7: <u>The Hunted Heart</u>

Book 7: <u>Wicked Wolf</u>

**The Elements of Five Series:**

Book 1: From Breath and Ruin

Book 2: From Flame and Ash

Book 3: From Spirit and Binding

Book 4: From Shadow and Silence

**Dante's Circle Series:**

Book 1: <u>Dust of My Wings</u>

Book 2: <u>Her Warriors' Three Wishes</u>

Book 3: <u>An Unlucky Moon</u>

Book 3.5: <u>His Choice</u>

Book 4: <u>Tangled Innocence</u>

Book 5: <u>Fierce Enchantment</u>

Book 6: <u>An Immortal's Song</u>

Book 7: <u>Prowled Darkness</u>

Book 8: Dante's Circle Reborn

**Holiday, Montana Series:**

Book 1: <u>Charmed Spirits</u>

Book 2: <u>Santa's Executive</u>

Book 3: <u>Finding Abigail</u>

Book 4: <u>Her Lucky Love</u>

Book 5: Dreams of Ivory

**The Branded Pack Series:**

**(Written with Alexandra Ivy)**

Book 1: <u>Stolen and Forgiven</u>

Book 2: <u>Abandoned and Unseen</u>

Book 3: <u>Buried and Shadowed</u>

# ABOUT THE AUTHOR

Carrie Ann Ryan is the New York Times and USA Today bestselling author of contemporary, paranormal, and young adult romance. Her works include the Montgomery Ink, Redwood Pack, Fractured Connections, and Elements of Five series, which have sold over 3.0 million books worldwide. She started writing while in graduate school for her advanced degree in chemistry and hasn't stopped since. Carrie Ann has written over seventy-five novels and novellas with more in the works. When she's not losing herself in her emotional and action-packed worlds, she's reading as much as she can while wrangling her clowder of cats who have more followers than she does.

www.CarrieAnnRyan.com

# FROM BITTERSWEET PROMISES

## LEIF

"Not only did you convince me to somehow go on a blind date, it became a double date. How on earth did you work this magic on me, cousin?" I asked Lake as she leaned against the pillar just inside the restaurant.

Lake grinned at me, her dark hair pulled away from her face. She had on this swingy black dress and looked as if she were excited, anxious, nervous, and happy all at the same time. Considering she was bouncing on her toes when usually Lake was calm, cool, and collected, was saying something. "I asked, and you said yes. Because you love me."

"I might love you because we're family, but I still think we're making a mistake." I shook my head and pulled at my shirt sleeves. Lake had somehow convinced me to wear a button-up shirt tucked into gray pants, I even had on shiny shoes. I looked like a damn banker. But if that's what Lake wanted, that's what I would do.

Lake might technically be my cousin, even though we weren't blood-related, but we were more like brother and sister than any of my other cousins.

I had siblings, as did Lake, but with the generational gap, we were at least a decade older than all of our other cousins. That meant, despite the fact that we had lived over an hour apart for most of our lives, we'd grown up more like siblings.

I loved my three younger siblings and talked to them daily. Unlike some blended families, they *were* my brothers and sister and not like strangers or distant family members. I didn't feel a disconnect from the three of them, but Lake was still closer to me.

Probably because we were either heading into our thirties or already there, where most of our other cousins were either just now in their early twenties or still teenagers in high school. With how big we Montgomerys were as a family, it made sense that there would be such a widespread age group.

That meant that Lake and I were best friends, cousins, practically siblings, and sometimes the banes of each other's existences.

We were also business owners and partners and saw each other too often these days. That was probably why she convinced me to go on a blind double date. But she had been out with Zach before. I, however, had never met May. Lake had some connection with her that I wasn't sure about, and for some reason Lake's date had said yes to this double date.

And, in the complicated way of family, I had agreed to it. I must have been tired. Or perhaps I'd had too many beers. Because I didn't do blind dates, and recently, I didn't do dates at all.

Lake scanned her phone, then looked up at me, all innocence in her smart gaze. "You shouldn't have told me you wanted to settle down in your old age."

I narrowed my eyes. "I'm still in my early thirties, jerk. Stop calling me old."

"I shouldn't call you old since you're only a few years older than me." She fluttered her eyelashes and I flipped her off, ignoring the stare from the older woman next to me. Though I was a tattoo artist, I didn't have many visible tattoos. Most of mine were on my back and legs, hidden from the world unless I wanted to show them. I hadn't figured out what I wanted on my arms beyond a few small pieces on my wrists and upper shoulders. And since tattoos were permanent, I was taking my time. If a client needed to see my skin with ink to feel comfortable, I'd show them my back. My body was a canvas, so I did what I could to set people at ease.

But I still had the eyebrow piercing and had recently taken out my nose ring. I didn't look too scary for most people. But apparently, flipping off a woman, growling, and cursing a time or two in front of strangers probably made me appear too close to the dark side.

"Yes, I want to settle down, but this will be awkward, won't it? Where the two of us are strangers, and the two of you aren't?" I wanted a life, a future, and yeah, one day to settle down with someone. I just didn't know why I'd mentioned it to Lake in the first place.

"If it helps, May doesn't know Zach, either. So it's a group of strangers, except I know everybody." She clapped her hands together and did her version of an evil laugh, and I just shook my head.

"Considering what you do for a living and how you like to manipulate things in your way, this makes sense. Are you going to be adding a matchmaking company to your conglomerate?"

Lake just fluttered her eyelashes again and laughed. Lake owned a small tech company that made a shit ton of money over the past couple of years. And because she was brilliant at what she did, innovative, and liked pushing money towards women-owned businesses, she owned more than one company at this point and was an investor in mine. I wouldn't be surprised if she found a way to open up a women-owned matchmaking company right here in town.

"It might be fun. I can call it Montgomery Links." Her eyes went wide. "Oh, my God. I have to write that down." She pulled out her phone, began to take notes, and I pinched the bridge of my nose.

"You know I trust you with my actual life, but I don't know if I trust you with my dating life."

Lake tossed her hair behind her shoulder as she continued to type. "Shut up. You love me. And once I finish setting you up, the rest of the family's next."

"Oh, really? You're going to get Daisy and Noah next?" I asked, speaking of two more of our cousins.

"Maybe. Of course, Sebastian's the only one of the younger group that seems to have a serious girlfriend."

I nodded, speaking of our other familial business partner. Sebastian was still a teenager, though in college. He had wanted to open up Montgomery Ink Legacy with me, the full title of our company. There was a legacy to it, and Sebastian had wanted in. So, though he didn't work there full-time, he was putting his future towards us. And in the ways of young love, he and his girlfriend had been together since middle school. The fact that my younger cousin was better at relationships than I was didn't make me feel great. But I was going to ignore that.

"You're not going to start up a matchmaking service, are you? Or maybe an app?"

"Dating apps are ridiculous these days, they practically want you to invest in coins to bid on dates, and that's not something I'm in the mood for. But maybe there's something I can try. I'll add it to my list."

Lake's list of inventions and tech was notorious, and knowing the brilliance of my cousin, she would one day rule the world and might eventually cross everything off that list.

"Oh, here's Zach." Lake's face brightened immediately, and she smiled up at a man with dark hair, piercing gray eyes, and an actual dimple on his cheek.

Tonight was not only about my blind date, but me getting the lay of the land when it came to Zach. I was the first step into meeting the family. Oh, if Zach passed my gauntlet, he would meet the rest of the Montgomerys, and we were mighty. All one hundred of us.

"Zach, you're here." Lake's voice went soft, and she went on her tiptoes even in her high heels as Zach pressed a soft kiss to her lips.

"Of course, I'm here. And you're early, as usual."

Lake blushed and ducked her head. "Well, you know me. I like to be early because being on time is late," she said at the same time I did, mumbling under my breath. It was a familiar refrain when it came to us.

"Zach, good to meet you," I said, holding out my hand.

The other man gripped it firmly and shook. "Nice to meet you too, Leif. I know you might be the one on a blind date soon, but I'm nervous."

I chuckled, shaking my head. "Yeah, I'm pretty nervous too. Though I'm grateful that Lake's trying to look out for me."

My cousin laughed softly. "You totally were not saying that a few minutes ago, but be suave and sophisticated now. Or just be yourself, May's on her way."

I met Zach's gaze and we both rolled our eyes. When I turned toward the door, I saw a woman of average height, with black straight hair, green eyes, and a sweet smile. I didn't know much about May, other than Lake knew her and liked her. If I was going to start dating again after taking time off to get the rest of my life together, I might as well start with someone that one of my best friends liked.

"May, I'm so glad that you're here," Lake said as she hugged the other woman tightly.

As Lake began to bounce on her heels, I realized that my cousin's cool, calm, and collected exterior was only for work. She was bouncing and happy when it came to her friends or when she was nervous. I knew that, of course, but I had forgotten how she had turned into the mogul that she was. It was good to see her relaxed and happy.

Now I just needed to figure out how to do that for myself.

May stood in front of me, and I felt like I was starting middle school all over again. A new school, a new life, and a past that didn't make much sense to anyone else.

I swallowed hard and nodded, not putting out my

hand to shake, thinking that would be weird, but I also didn't want to hug her. I didn't even know this woman. Why was everything so awkward? Instead, I lifted my chin. "Hello, May. It's nice to meet you. Lake says only good things."

There, smooth. Not really. Zach began to move out of frame, with Lake at his side as the two went to speak to the hostess, leaving May and me alone.

This wasn't going to be awkward at all.

The woman just smiled at me, her eyes wide. "It's nice to meet you, too. And Lake does speak highly of you. Also, this is very awkward, so I'm so sorry if I say something stupid. I know that your cousin said that I should be set up with you which is great but I'm not great at blind dates and apparently this is a double date and now I'm going to stop talking." She said the words so quickly they all ran into one breath.

I shook my head and laughed. "We're on the same page there."

"Okay, good. It's nice to meet you, Leif Montgomery."

"And it's nice to meet you too, May."

We made our way to Lake and Zach, who had gotten our table, and we all sat down, talking about work and other things. May was in child life development, taught online classes, and was also a nanny.

"I'm actually about to start with a new family soon. I'm excited. I know that being a nanny isn't something that most people strive for, or at least that's what they tell you, but I love being able to work with children and be the person that is there when a single parent or even both parents are out in the workforce, trying to do everything."

I nodded, taking a sip of my beer. "I get you completely. With how my parents worked, I was lucky that they were able to get childcare within the buildings. Since they each owned their own businesses, they made it work. But my family worked long hours, and that's why I ended up being the babysitter a lot of the times when childcare wasn't an option." I cleared my throat. "I'm a lot older than a lot of my cousins," I added.

"Both of us are, but I'm glad that you only said yourself," Lake said, grinning. She leaned into Zach as she spoke, the four of us in a horseshoe-shaped booth. That gave May and me space since this was a first date and still awkward as hell, and so Lake and Zach could cuddle. Not that that was something I needed to be a part of.

"Oh, I'm glad that you didn't judge. The last few

dates that I've been on they always gave me weird looks because I think they expected a nanny to be this old crone or someone that's looking for a different job." She shrugged and continued. "When I eventually get married and maybe even start a family, I want to continue my job. I like being there to help another family achieve their goals. And I can't believe I just said start a family on my first date. And that I mentioned that I've been on a few other dates." She let out a breath. "I'm notoriously bad at dating. Like, the worst. Just warning you."

I laughed, shaking my head. "I'm rusty at it, so don't worry." And even though I said that, I had a feeling that May felt no spark towards me, and I didn't feel anything towards her. She was nice and pleasant, and I could probably consider her a friend one day. But there wasn't any spark. May's eyes weren't dancing. She wasn't leaning forward, trying to touch my hand across the table. We were just sitting there casually, enjoying a really good steak, as Lake and Zach enjoyed their date.

By the end of dinner, I didn't want dessert, and neither did May, so we said goodbye to the other couple, who decided to stay. I walked May to her car, ignoring Lake's warning look, but I didn't know what exactly she was warning me about.

"Thanks for dinner," May said. "I could have paid. I know this is a blind date and all that, but you didn't have to pay."

I shook my head. "I paid for the four of us because I wanted to be nice. I'll make Lake pay next time."

May beamed. "Yes, I like that. You guys are a good family."

"Anyway," I said, clearing my throat as I stuck my hands in my pockets. "I guess I'll see you around."

May just looked at me, threw her head back, and laughed. "You're right. You are rusty at this."

"Sorry." Heat flushed my skin, and I resisted the urge to tug on my eyebrow ring.

"It's okay. No spark. I'm used to it. I don't spark well."

"May, I'm sorry." I cringed. "It's not you."

"Oh, God, please don't say that. 'It's not you. It's me. You're working on yourself. You're just so busy with work.' I've heard it all."

"Seriously?" I asked. May was hot. Nice, but there just wasn't a spark.

She shrugged. "It's okay. I'll probably see you around sometime because I am friends with Lake. However, I am perfectly fine having this be our one and only. You'll find your person. It's okay that it's not me." And with that, she got in the car and left, leaving me standing there.

Well then. Tonight wasn't horrible, but it wasn't great. I got in my car, and instead of heading home where I'd be alone, watching something on some streaming service while I drank a beer and pretended that I knew what I was doing with my life, I headed into Montgomery Ink Legacy.

We were the third branch of the company and the first owned by our generation. Montgomery Ink was the tattoo shop in downtown Denver. While there were open spots for some walk-ins and special circumstances, my father, aunt, and their team had years' worth of waiting lists. They worked their asses off and made sure to get in everybody that they could, but people wanted Austin Montgomery's art. Same with my aunt, Maya.

There was another tattoo shop down in Colorado Springs, owned by my parents' cousins, who I just called aunt and uncle because we were close enough that using real titles for everybody got confusing. Montgomery Ink Too was thriving down there, and they had waiting lists as well. My family could have opened more shops and gone nationwide, even global if they wanted to, but they liked keeping it how it was, in the family and those connected.

We were a branch, but our own in the making. I had gone into business with Lake, of course, and Sebastian, when he was ready, as well as Nick. Nick was my best friend. I had known him for ages, and he had wanted to be part of something as well. He might not be a Montgomery by name, but he had eaten over at my family's house enough times throughout the years that he was practically a Montgomery. And he had invested in the company as well, and so now we were nearly a year into owning the shop and trying not to fail.

I pulled into the parking lot, grateful it was still open since we didn't close until nine most nights, and greeted Nick, who was still working.

Sebastian was in the back, going over sketches with a client, and I nodded at him. He might be eighteen, but he was still in training, an apprentice, and was working his ass off to learn.

"Date sucked then?" Sebastian asked, and Nick just rolled his eyes and went back to work on a client's wrist.

"I don't want to talk about it," I groaned.

The rest of the staff was off since Nick would

close up on his own. Sebastian was just there since he didn't have homework or a date with Marley.

"Was she hot at least?" Sebastian asked, and the client, a woman in her sixties, bopped him on the head with her bag gently.

"Sebastian Montgomery. Be nice."

Sebastian blushed. "Sorry, Mrs. Anderson."

I looked over at the woman and grinned. "Hi, Mrs. Anderson. It's nice to see you out of the classroom."

She narrowed her eyes at me, even though they filled with laughter. "I needed my next Jane Austen tattoo, thank you very much," the older woman said as she went back to working with Sebastian. She had been my and then Sebastian's English teacher. The fact that she was on her fifth tattoo with some literary quote told me that I had been damn lucky in most of my teachers growing up.

She was kick-ass, and I had a feeling that she would let Sebastian do the tattoo for her rather than just have him work on the design with me as we did for most of the people who came in. He had learned under my father and was working under me now. It was strange to think that he wasn't a little kid anymore. But he was in a long-term relationship, kicking ass in college, and knew what he wanted to do with his life.

I might know what I want to do with my work life, but everything else seemed a little off.

"So it didn't work out?" Nick asked as he walked up to the front desk with the clients after going over aftercare.

"Not really," I said, looking down at my phone.

The client, a woman in her mid-twenties with bright pink hair, a lip ring, and kind eyes, leaned over the desk to look at me.

"You'll find someone, Leif. Don't worry."

I looked at our regular and shook my head. "Thanks, Kim. Too bad that you don't swing this way."

I winked as I said it, a familiar refrain from both of us.

Kim was married to a woman named Sonya, and the two of them were happy and working on in vitro with donated sperm for their first kid.

"Hey, I'm sorry too that I'm a lesbian. I'll never know what it means to have Leif Montgomery. Or any Montgomery, since I found my love far too quickly. I mean, what am I ever going to do not knowing the love of a Montgomery?"

Mrs. Anderson chuckled from her chair, Sebastian held back a snort, and I just looked at Nick, who rolled his eyes and helped Kim out of the place.

I was tired, but it was okay. The date wasn't all bad. May was nice. But it felt like I didn't have much right then.

And then Nick sat in front of me, scowled, and I realized that I did have something. I had my friends and my family. I didn't need much more.

"So, you and May didn't work out?"

I raised a brow. "You knew her name? Did I tell you that?"

Nick shook his head. "Lake did."

That made sense, considering the two of them spoke as much as we did. "So, was it your idea to set me up on a blind date?"

"Fuck no. That was all Lake. I just do what she says. Like we all do."

I sighed and went through my appointments for the next day. "We're busy for the next month. That's good, right?" I asked.

"You're the business genius here. I just play with ink. But yes, that's good. Now, don't let your cousin set you up any more dates. Find them for yourself. You know what you're doing."

"So says the man who dates less than me."

"That's what you think. I'm more private about it.

As it should be." I flipped him off as he stood up, then he gestured towards a stack of bills in the corner. "You have a few personal things that made their way here. Don't want you to miss out on them before you head home."

"Thanks, bro."

"No problem. I'm going to help Sebastian with his consult, and then I'll clean up. You should head home. Though you're doing it alone, so I feel sorry for you."

"Fuck you," I called out.

"Fuck you, too."

"Boys," Mrs. Anderson said, in that familiar English teacher refrain, and both Nick and I cringed before saying, "Sorry," simultaneously.

Sebastian snickered, then went back to work, and I headed towards the edge of the counter, picking up the stack of papers. Most were bills, some were random papers that needed to be filed or looked over. Some were just junk mail. But there was one letter, written in block print that didn't look familiar. Chills went up my spine and I opened it, wondering what the fuck this was. Maybe it was someone asking to buy my house. I got a lot of handwritten letters for that, but I didn't think this was going to be that. I swallowed hard, slid open the paper, and froze.

*"I'll find you, boy. Oops. Looks like I already did. Be waiting. I know you miss me."*

I let the paper hit the top of the counter and swallowed hard, trying to remain cool so I didn't worry anyone else.

I didn't know exactly who that was from, but I had a horrible feeling that they wouldn't wait long to tell me.

**Read the rest in Bittersweet Promises! OUT NOW!**

# FROM THE FOREVER RULE

## ASTON

*The Cages are the most prestigious family in Denver—at least according to the patriarch of the Cage Family.*
*And the Cages have rules.*
*Rules only they know.*

I always knew that one day my father would die. I hadn't realized that day would come so soon. Or that the last words I would say to him would've been in anger.

I had been having one of the best nights of my life, a beautiful woman in my arms, and a smile on my face when I received the phone call that had changed my family's life.

The fact that I had been smiling had been a shock, because according to my brothers, I didn't smile much. I was far too busy being *The Cage* of Cage Enterprises.

We were a dominant force in the city of Denver when it came to certain real estate ventures, as well as being one of the only ethical and environmentally friendly ones who tried to keep up with that. We had our hands in countless different pots around the world, but mostly we gravitated in the state of Colorado—our home.

I had not created the company, no, that honor had gone to my grandfather, and then my father. The Cage Enterprises were and would always be a family endeavor. And when my father had stepped away a few years ago, stating he had wanted to see the world, and also see if his sons could actually take up the mantle, I had stepped in—not that the man believed we could.

My brothers were in various roles within the company, at least those who had wanted to be part of it. But I was the face of Cage Enterprises.

So no, I hadn't smiled often. There wasn't time. We weren't billionaires with mega yachts. We worked seventy-hour weeks to make sure *all* our employees had a livable wage while wining and dining with those who looked down at us for not being on their level. And others thought we were the high and mighty anyway since they didn't understand us. So, I didn't smile.

But I had smiled that night.

It had been a gala for some charity, one I couldn't even remember off the top of my head. We had donated between the company and my own finances —we always did. But I couldn't even remember anything about why we were there.

Yet I could remember her smile. The heat in her eyes when she had looked up at me, the feel of her body pressed against mine as we had danced along the dance floor, and then when we ended up in the hallway, bodies pressed against one another, needing each other, wanting each other.

And I had put aside all my usual concepts of business and life to have this woman in my arms.

And then my mother had called and had shattered that illusion.

"Your father is dead."

She hadn't even braced me for the blow. A heart attack on a vacation on a beach in Majorca, and he was dead. She hadn't cried, hadn't said anything, just told me that I had to be the one to tell my brothers.

And so, I had, all six of them. Because of course

Loren Cage would have seven sons. He couldn't do things just once, he had to make sure he left his legacy, his destiny.

And that was why we were here today, in a high-rise in Centennial, waiting on my father's lawyer to show up with the reading of the will.

"Hey, when is Winstone going to get here?" Dorian asked, his typical high energy playing on his face, and how he tapped his fingers along the hand-carved wooden table.

I stared at my brother, at those piercing blue eyes that matched my own, and frowned. He should be here soon. He did call us all here after all."

"I still don't know why we all had to be here for the reading of the will," Hudson whispered as he stared off into the distance. Neither Dorian nor Hudson worked for Cage Enterprises. They had stock with the company, and a few other connections because that's what family did, but they didn't work on the same floors as some of us and hadn't been elbow to elbow with our father before he had retired. Though dear old dad had worked in our small town more often than not in the end. In fact, Hudson didn't even live in Denver anymore. He had moved to the town we owned in the mountains.

Because of course we Cages owned a damned

town. Part of me wasn't sure if the concept of having our name on everything within the town had been on purpose or had occurred organically. Though knowing my grandfather, perhaps it had been exactly what he'd wanted. He had bought up a few buildings, built a few more, and now we owned three-quarters of the town, including the major resort which brought in tourists and income.

And that was why we were here.

"You have to be here because you're evidently in the will," I said softly, trying not to get annoyed that we were waiting for our father's lawyer. Again.

"You would think he would be able to just send us a memo. I mean, it should be clear right? We all know what stakes we have in, we should just be able to do things evenly," Theo said, his gaze off into the distance. My younger brother also didn't work for the company, instead he had decided to go to culinary school, something my father had hated. But you couldn't control a Cage, that was sort of our deal.

"Why would you be cut out of the will?" I asked, honestly curious.

"Because I married a man and a woman," he drawled out. "You know he hasn't spoken to me since before the wedding," Ford said, and I saw the hurt in his gaze even though I knew he was probably trying to hide it.

"Well, he was an asshole, what do you expect?" James asked.

I looked behind Ford to see my brother and co-chair of Cage Enterprises standing with his hands in his pockets, staring out the window.

With Flynn, our vice president, standing beside him, they looked like the heads of businesses they were. While they wore suits and so did I, we were the only ones.

Dorian and Hudson were both in jeans, Hudson's having a hole at the knee. And probably not as a fashion statement, most likely because it had torn at some point, and he hadn't bothered to buy another pair. Theo was in slacks, but a Henley with his sleeves pushed up, tapping his finger just like Hudson, clearly wanting to get out of here as well. Ford had on cargo pants, and a tight black T-shirt, and looked like he had just gotten off his shift. He owned a security company with his husband and a few other friends, and did security for the Cages when he could, though I knew he didn't like to work with family often. And I knew it wasn't because of us. No, it was Father—even if he had officially *retired*. It was always Father.

And he was gone.

"Can't believe the asshole's gone," I whispered.

Ford's brows rose. "Look at that, you calling him an asshole. I'm proud."

"You should show him respect," Mother said as she came inside the room, her high heels tapping against the marble floors. I didn't bother standing up like I normally would have, because Melanie Cage looked to be in a *mood*.

She didn't look sad that Dad was gone, more like angry that he would dare go against their plans. What plans? I didn't know, but that was my mother.

She came right up to Dorian and leaned down to kiss his cheek. She didn't even bother to look at the rest of us. Dorian was Mother's favorite. Which I knew Dorian resented, but I didn't have to deal with mommy issues at this moment.

No, we had to deal with father issues at this point.

"I'm going to go get him," Flynn replied, turning toward the door. "I'm really not in the mood to wait any longer, especially since he's being so secretive about this meeting."

As I had been thinking just the same, I nodded at Flynn though he didn't need my permission. However, just then, the door opened, and I frowned when it wasn't just Mr. Winstone walking into the conference room.

I stared as an older woman walked through the door following Mr. Winstone, and four women and another man with messy hair and tattered cut-up jeans that matched Hudson's walked behind them.

The guy looked familiar, as if I'd seen him somewhere, or maybe it was just his eyes.

Where had I seen those eyes before?

"Phoebe? What are you doing here?" Ford asked as he moved forward and gripped the hands of one of the women.

"I was going to ask the same question," Phoebe asked as she looked at Ford, then around the room.

Those of us sitting stood up, confused about why this other family—because they were clearly a family—had decided to enter the room.

"We're here to meet the lawyer about my father's death, Ford. Why would you and the Cages be here?" she asked, and I wondered how the hell Mr. Winstone had fucked up so badly? Why the hell was he letting another family that clearly seemed to be in shock come into our room? This wasn't how he normally handled things.

Ford was the one who answered though—thankfully—because I had no idea what the hell was going on.

"Phoebe, we're here for my dad's will reading. What the hell is going on?" he asked. Phoebe looked around, as well as the others.

I stared at them, at the tall willowy one with wide eyes, at the smaller one with tears still in her eyes as if she was the only one truly mourning, and at the woman who seemed to be in charge, not the mother. Instead she had shrewd eyes and was glaring at all of us. The man stood back, hands in pockets, and looked just as shell-shocked as Ford.

But before Mr. Winstone or anyone else could say anything, my mother spoke in such a crisp, icy tone that I froze.

"I don't know why you're acting so dramatic. You knew your father was an asshole. He just liked creating drama," she snapped.

As I tried to catch up with her words, the older woman answered. "Melanie, stop."

This couldn't be happening. Because things started to click into place. The fact that the man at the other end of this table had our eyes, and that everybody looked so fucking shocked. I didn't know how Ford knew this Phoebe, and I would be getting answers.

"We had a deal," my mother continued, as it seemed that the rest of us were just now catching on. "You would keep your family away from mine. We would share Loren, but I got the name, I got the family. You got whatever else. But now it looks like Loren decided to be an asshole again."

"What are you talking about?" the shrewd sister asked as she came forward, her hands fisted at her side.

"Excuse me," I said, clearing my throat. I was going to be damned if I let anyone else handle this meeting. I was The Cage now. "Will someone please explain?"

"Well, I wasn't quite sure how this was going to work out," Mr. Winstone began, and we all quieted, while I wanted to strangle the man. What did he mean how *the hell this would work out*? What was this?

This seemed like a big fucking mistake.

"Loren Cage had certain provisions in his will for both of his families. And one of the many requirements that I will go over today is that this meeting must take place." He paused and I hoped it wasn't for effect, because I was going to throttle him if it was. "Loren Cage had two families. Seven sons with his wife Melanie, and four daughters and a son with his mistress, Constance."

"We went by partner," the other mother corrected.

I blinked, counting the adults in the room. "Twelve?" I asked, my voice slightly high-pitched.

"Busy fucking man," Dorian whispered.

Hudson snorted, while we just stood and stared at each other.

*This could not be happening. A secret family? No, we were not that cliché.*

"I can't do this," Phoebe blurted, her eyes wide.

"Oh, stop overreacting," my mother scorned.

"Do not talk to my daughter that way." The other mother glared.

"It was always going to be an issue," Mother continued. "All the secrets and the lies. And now the kids will have to deal with it. Because God forbid Loren ever deal with anything other than his own dick."

"That's enough," I snapped.

"Don't you dare talk to us like that," the shrewd sister snapped right back.

"I will talk however I damn well please. I am going to need to know exactly how this happened," I shouted over everyone else's words.

Out of the corner of my eye I saw Phoebe run

through the door. Ford followed and then the tall willowy one joined.

"Shit," I snapped.

"Language," Mother bit out.

I laughed. "Really? You are going to talk to me about language."

I looked over at James, who shrugged, before he put two fingers in his mouth and whistled that high-pitched whistle that only he could do.

Everyone froze as Theo rubbed his ear and glared at me.

"Winstone," I said through gritted teeth. "I take it we all have to be here in order for this to happen?"

He cleared his throat. "At least a majority. But you all had to at least step into the room."

"Excuse me then," I said.

"You're just going to leave? Just like that?" my mother asked.

I whirled on her. "I'm going to go see if my apparent *family* is okay. Then I'm going to come back and we're going to get answers. Because there is no way that I'm going to leave here without them."

I stormed out the door, and thankfully nobody followed me.

Of course, though, I shouldn't have been too swift with that, as the woman who had to be the eldest sister practically ran to my side, her heels tapping against the marble.

"I'm coming with you."

"That's just fine." I paused, knowing that I wasn't angry at these people. No, my father and apparently our mothers were the ones that had to deal with this. I looked over at the woman who Mr. Winstone and the mothers had claimed was my sister and cleared my throat.

"I'm Aston."

"Is this really the time for introductions?" she asked.

"I'm about to go see your sister and my brother to make sure that they're fine, so sure. I would like to know the name of the woman that is running next to me right now."

"I'm running, you're walking quickly because you have such long legs."

I snorted, surprised I could even do that.

"I'm Isabella," she replied after a moment.

"I would say nice to meet you Isabella…" I let my voice trail off.

She let out a sharp laugh before shaking her head. "I'm going to need a moment to wrap my head around this, but not now."

"Same."

We stormed out of the building, and I lagged behind since Ford was standing in front of Phoebe who was in the arms of another man with dark hair and everybody seemed to be talking all at once.

"I just. I can't deal with this right now," Phoebe said, and I realized that something else must have been going on with her right then. She looked tired, and far more emotional than the rest of us.

I looked over at the man holding her and blinked. "Kane?" I asked.

Kane stared at me and let out a breath. "Wow," he said with a laugh.

"We'll handle it," Isabella put in, completely ignoring us. "And if we need to meet again later, we will." Then she looked over at Ford and I, with such menace in her gaze, I nearly took a step back. "Is that a problem?"

I raised my chin, glaring right back at her. "Not at all. However I want answers, so I'd rather not have the meeting canceled right now. But I'm also not going to force any of my," I paused, realization hitting far too hard, "*family* to stay if they don't want to."

And with that, I turned on my heel and went back into the building, with Isabella and Ford following me. Everyone was still yelling in the interim, and I cleared my throat. As Isabella had done it at the same time, everyone paused to look at me.

"Read the damn will. Because we need answers," I ordered Winstone, and he shook like a leaf before nodding.

"Okay. We can do that." He cleared his throat, then he began going over trusts and incomes and buildings and things that I would care about soon, but what I wanted to know was what the hell our father had been thinking about.

"Here's the tricky part," Winstone began, as we all leaned forward, eager to hear what the hell he had to say.

"The family money, not of the business, not of each of your inheritance from other family members, but the bulk of Loren Cage's assets will be split between all twelve kids."

"Are you kidding me?" Isabella asked. "What money? We weren't exactly poor, but we were solidly middle class."

"We did just fine," the other mother pleaded.

My mother snorted, clearly not believing the words.

I glared at the woman who raised me, willing her to say *anything*. She would probably be pushed out of the window at that point. Not by me, by someone else, but she probably would've earned it.

The lawyer continued. "However to retain the majority of current assets and to keep Cage Lake and all of its subsidiaries you will have to meet as a family once a month for three years. If this does not happen, Cage Enterprises will be broken into multiple parts and sold." He went on into the legalese that I ignored as I tried to hear over the blood pounding in my ears.

"You own a town?" the other man asked.

I looked over at the one man in the room I didn't know the name of. "Not exactly."

"Kyler," Isabella whispered.

In that moment, I realized that I had a brother named Kyler—if this was all to be believed.

"This can't be legal right?" the tall willowy person said.

"Yes Sophia, it can," their mother put in.

Oh good, another sister named Sophia.

*Only one name to go.* What the hell was wrong with me?

I forced my jaw to relax. "Are you telling us that we need to have all twelve of us at dinner once a month for three years in order to keep what is rightly inherited to us? To keep people in business and keep their jobs?"

"We don't need the money, but everyone else in our employ does," James snapped. "As do those we work with."

"Damn straight," Dorian growled.

"How are we supposed to believe this?" I asked, asking the obvious question.

"First, only five must attend, and two must be of a different family." The lawyer continued as if I hadn't spoken. "Of course you are *all* family…"

"Again, how are we supposed to believe this?" I asked.

"Here are the DNA tests already done."

"Are you fucking kidding me?" Isabella asked.

I looked at her, as she had literally taken the words out of my mouth.

"Isn't that sort of like a violation?" Kyler asked, his face pale.

"We need to get our own lawyers on this," James whispered.

I nodded tightly, knowing we had much more to say on this.

"There's no way this is legal," the youngest said, and I looked over at her.

"What's your name?" I asked.

"Emily. Emily Cage Dixon," she said softly, and we all froze.

"Your middle name is Cage?" I asked, biting out the words.

"All of our middle names are Cage," Sophia said, shaking her head. "I hated it but Dad wanted to be cute because our father's name was Cage Dixon, or maybe it wasn't. Is he also a bigamist?" she asked.

Her mother lifted her chin. "We never married. And no, your father's name was not Dixon, that was my maiden name."

"What?" Sophia asked. "All this time...are our grandparents even dead?"

"Yes, my parents are dead. The same with Loren's." The other mother's eyes filled with tears. "I'm sorry we lied."

"We'll get to that later," Isabella put in, and I was grateful.

I let out a breath. "In order to keep our assets, in order to keep the family name intact, we need to have *dinner*. For three years."

The small lawyer nodded, his glasses falling down his nose. "At least five of you. And it can start three months after the funeral, which we can plan after this."

"This is ridiculous," Hudson murmured under his breath, before he got up and walked out.

I watched him go, knowing he had his own demons, and tried to understand what the hell was going on. "Why did he do this?" I asked, more to myself than anyone else.

"I never really knew the man, but apparently none of us did," Isabella said, staring off into the distance.

"Leave the paperwork and go," I ordered Winstone, and he didn't even mutter a peep. Instead, he practically ran out of the room. James and Flynn immediately went to the paperwork, and I knew they were scouring it. But from the way that their jaws tightened, I had a feeling that my father had found a way to make this legal. Because we would always have a choice to lose everything. That was the man.

"It's true," my mother put in. "You all share the same father. That was the deal when we got married, and when he decided to bring this other woman into our lives."

"I'm pretty sure you were the other woman," the other mom said.

I pinched the bridge of my nose.

"Stop. All of you." I stared at the group and realized that I was probably the eldest Cage here, other than the moms. I would deal with this. We didn't have a choice. "Whatever happens, we'll deal with it."

"You're in charge now?" Isabella asked, but Sophia shushed her.

I was grateful for that, because I had a feeling Isabella and I were going to butt heads more often than not.

I shrugged, trying to act as if my world hadn't been rocked. "I would say welcome to the Cages, because DNA evidence seems to point that way, however perhaps you were already one of us all along."

Kyler muttered something under his breath I couldn't hear before speaking up. "You have my eyes," he said.

I nodded. "Noticed that too."

The other man tilted his head. "So what, we do dinners and we make nice?"

I sighed. "We don't have to be adversaries."

"You say that as if you're the one in charge," Isabella said again.

"Because he is," Theo said, and they all stared at him.

I tried to tamp down the pride swelling at those words—along with the overwhelming pressure.

Theo continued. "He's the eldest. He's the one that takes care of us. And he's the CEO of Cage Enterprises. He's going to be the one that deals with the paperwork fallout."

"Because family is just paperwork?" Emily asked, her voice lost.

I shook my head. "No, family is insane, and apparently, it's been secret all along. And it looks like we have a few introductions to make, and a few tests to redo. But if it turns out it's true, we're Cages, and we don't back down."

"And what does that mean?" Isabella asked, her tone far too careful.

Theo was the one who finally answered. "It means we're going to have to figure shit out."

And for just an instant, the thought of that beautiful woman with that gorgeous smile came to mind, and I pushed those thoughts away. My family was breaking, or perhaps breaking open. And I didn't have time to worry about things like a woman who had made me smile.

The Cages needed me and after today's meeting there would be no going back to sanity.

Ever.


**In the mood to read another family saga? Meet the
Cage Family in The Forever Rule!**

# FROM ONE WAY BACK TO ME

## ELI

When my morning begins with me standing ankle-deep in a basement full of water, I know I probably should have stayed in bed. Only, I was the boss, and I didn't get that choice.

"Hold on. I'm looking for it." East cursed underneath his breath as my younger brother bent down around the pipe, trying his best to turn off the valve. I sighed, waded through the muck in my work boots, and moved to help him. "I said I've got it," East snapped, but I ignored him.

I narrowed my eyes at the evil pipe. "It's old and rusted, and even though it passed an inspection over a year ago, we knew this was going to be a problem."

"And I'm the fucking handyman of this company. I've got this."

"And as a handyman, you need a hand."

"You're hilarious. Seriously. I don't know how I could ever manage without your wit and humor." The dryness in his tone made my lips twitch even as I did my best to ignore the smell of whatever water we stood in.

"Fuck you," I growled.

"No thanks. I'm a little too busy for that."

With a grunt, East shut off the water, and we both stood back, hands on our hips as we stared at the mess of this basement.

East let out a sigh. "I'm not going to have to turn the water off for the whole property, but I'm glad that we don't have tenants in this particular cabin."

I nodded tightly and held back a sigh. "This is probably why there aren't basements in Texas. Because everything seems to go wrong in these things."

"I'm pretty sure this is a storm shelter, or at least a tornado one. Not quite sure as it's one of the only basements in the area."

"It was probably the only one that they had the energy to make back in the day. Considering this whole place is built over clay and limestone."

East nodded, looked around. "I'll start the cleanup with this water, and we'll look to see what we can do with the pipes."

I pinched the bridge of my nose. "I don't want to have to replace the plumbing for this whole place."

"At least it's not the villa itself, or the farmhouse, or the winery. Just a single cabin."

I glared at my younger brother, then reached out and knocked on a wooden pillar. "Shut your mouth. Don't say things like that to me. We are just now getting our feet under us."

East shrugged. "It's the truth, though. However much you weigh it, it could have been worse."

I pinched the bridge of my nose. "Jesus Christ. You were in the military for how long? A Wilder your entire life, and you say things like that? When the hell did you lose that superstition bone?"

"About the time that my Humvee was blown up, and when Evan's was, Everett's too. Hell, about the time that you almost fell out of the sky in your plane. Or when Elliot was nearly shot to death trying to help one of his men. So, yes, I pretty much lost all superstition when trying to toe the line ended up in near death and maiming."

I met my brother's gaze, that familiar pang

thinking about all that we had lost and almost lost over the past few years.

East muttered under his breath, shaking his head. "And I sound more and more like Evan these days rather than myself."

I squeezed his shoulder and let out a breath, thinking of our brother who grunted more than spoke these days. "It's okay. We've been through a lot. But we're here."

Somehow, we were here. I wasn't quite sure if we had made the right decision about two years ago when we had formed this plan, or rather *I* had formed this plan, but there was no going back. We were in it, and we were going to have to find a way to make it work, flooded former tornado shelters and all.

East sighed. "I'll work on this now. Then I'll head on over to the main house. I have a few things to work on there."

"You know, we can hire you help. I know we had all the contractors and everything to work with us for some of the rebuilds and rehabs, but we can hire someone else for you on a day-to-day basis."

My brother shook his head. "We may be able to afford it, but I'd rather save that for a rainy day. Because when it rains, it pours here, and flash flooding is a major threat in this part of Texas." He winked as he said it, mixing his metaphors, and I just shook my head.

"You just let me know if you need it."

"You're the CEO, brother of mine, not the CFO. That's Everett."

"True, but we did talk about it so we can work on it." I paused, thinking about what other expenses might show up. "And what do you need to do with the villa?"

The villa was the main house where most things happened on the property. It contained the lobby, library, and atrium. My apartment was also on the top floor, so I could be there for emergencies. Our innkeeper lived on the other side of the house, but I was in the main loft because this was my project, my baby.

My other brothers, all five of them, lived in cabins on the property. We lived together, worked together, ate together, and fought together. We were the Wilder brothers. It was what we did.

I had left to join the Air Force at seventeen, having graduated early, leaving behind my kid brothers and sister. After nearly twenty years of doing what we needed to in order to survive, we hadn't spent as much time with one another as I would have liked. We hadn't been stationed together, so we hadn't seen one another for longer than holidays or in passing.

But now we were together. At least most of us. So I was going to make this work, even if it killed me.

East finally answered my question. "I just have to fix a door that's a little too squeaky in one of the guestrooms. Not a big deal."

I raised a brow. "That's it?"

"It's one of the many things on my list. Thankfully, this place is big enough that I always have something to do. It's an unending list. And that the winery has its own team to work on all of that shit, because I'm not in the mood to learn to deal with any of the complicated machinery that comes with that world."

I snorted. "Honestly, same. I'm glad there are people that know what the fuck they're doing when it comes to wine making so that didn't have to be the two of us."

I left my brother to this job, knowing he liked time on his own, just like the rest of us did, and went to dry my boots. I was working by myself for most of the day, in interviews and other "boss business," as Elliot called it, so I had to focus and get clean.

I wasn't in the mood to deal with interviews, but

it was part of my job. We had to fill positions that hadn't been working out over the past year, some more than others.

Wilder Retreat was a place that hadn't been even a spark in my mind my entire life. No, I had been too busy being a career military man—getting in my twenty, moving up the ranks, and ending up as a Lieutenant Colonel before I got out. I had been a commander of a squadron, and yet, it felt like I didn't know how to command where I was now.

When my sister Eliza had lost her husband when he was on deployment, it had been the last domino to fall in the Wilder brothers' military career. I had been ready to get out with twenty years in, knowing I needed a career outside of being a Lieutenant Colonel. I wasn't even forty yet, and the term retirement was a misnomer, but that's what happened when it came to my former job.

East had been getting out around that time for reasons of his own, and then Evan had been forced to. I rubbed my hand over my chest, that familiar pain, remembering the phone call from one of Evan's commanders when Evan had been hurt.

I thought I'd lost my baby brother then, and we nearly had. Everett had gotten hurt too, and Elijah and Elliot had needed out for their own reasons.

Losing our baby sister's husband had just pushed us forward.

Finding out that Eliza's husband had been a cheating asshole had just cemented the fact that we needed to spend more time together as a family so we could be there for one another.

In retrospect, it would have been nice if Eliza would have been able to come down to Texas with us, to our suburb outside of San Antonio. Only, she had fallen in love again, with a man with a big family and a good heart up in Fort Collins, Colorado. She was still up there and traveled down enough that we actually got to get to know our sister again.

It was weird to think that, after so many years of always seeing each other in passing or through video calls, most of us were here, opening up a business. And all because I had been losing my mind.

Wilder Retreat and Winery was a villa and wedding venue outside of San Antonio. We were in hill country, at least what passed for hill country in South Texas, and the place had been owned by a former Air Force General who had wanted to retire and sell the place, since his kid didn't want it.

It was a large spread that used to be a ranch back in the day, nearly one hundred acres that the original owners had taken from a working ranch, and instead of making it a dude ranch or something similar, like others did around here, they'd added a winery using local help. We were close enough to Fredericksburg that it made sense in terms of the soil and weather. They had been able to add on additions, so it wasn't just the winery. Someone could come for the day for a winery tour or even a retreat tour, but most people came for the weekend or for a whole week. There were cabins and a farmhouse where we held weddings, dances, or other events. We had some chickens and ducks that gave us eggs, and goats that seemed to have a mind of their own and provided milk for cheese. Then there was the main annex, which housed all the equipment for the retreat villa.

The winery had its own section of buildings, and it was far bigger than anything I would have ever thought that we could handle. But, between the six of us, we did.

And the only reason we could even afford it, because one didn't afford something like this on a military salary, even with a decent retirement plan, was because of our uncles.

Our uncles, Edward and Edmond Wilder, had owned Wilder Wines down in Napa, California, for years. They had done well for themselves, and when we had been kids, we had gone out to visit. Evan had been the one that had clung to it and had been interested in wine making before he had changed his mind and gone into the military like the rest of us.

That was why Evan was in charge of the winery itself now. Because he knew what he was doing, even if he'd growled and said he didn't. Either way though, the place was huge, had multiple working parts at all times, and we had a staff that needed us. But when the uncles had died, they had left the money from the sale of the winery to us in equal parts. Eliza had taken hers to invest for her future children, and the rest of us had pooled our money together to buy this place and make it ours. A lot of the staff from the old owner had stayed, but some had left as well. Because they didn't want new owners who had no idea what they were doing, or they just retired. Either way, we were over a year in and doing okay.

Except for two positions that made me want to groan.

I had an interview with who would be our third wedding planner since we started this. The main component of the retreat was to have an actual wedding venue. To be able to host parties, and not just wine tours. Elliot was our major event planner that helped with our yearly and seasonal minute details, but he didn't want anything to do with the actual weddings. That was a whole other skill set, and so we wanted a wedding planner. We had gone through two wedding planners now, and we needed to hire a third. The first one had lied on her résumé, had given references that were her friends who had lied and had even created websites that were all fabrication, all so she could get into the business. Which, I understood, getting into the business is one thing. However, lying was another. Plus, we needed someone with actual experience because we didn't have any ourselves. We were going out on a limb here with this whole retreat business, and it was all because I had the harebrained idea of getting our family to work together, get along, and get to know one another. I wanted us to have a future, to be our own bosses.

And it was so far over my head that I knew that if I didn't get reliable help, we were going to fail.

Later, I had a meeting with that potential wedding planner. But first, I had to see what the fuck that smell was coming from the main kitchen in the villa.

The second wedding planner we hired was a guy with great and *true* references, one who was good at his job but hated everything to do with my brothers and me. He had hated the idea of the retreat and how rustic it was, even though we were in fucking South Texas. Yes, the buildings look slightly European because that was the theme that the original owners had gone for. Still, the guy had hated us, hadn't listened to us, and had called us white trash before he had walked away, jumped into his convertible, and sped off down the road, leaving us without help. He had been rude to our guests, and now Elliot was the one having to plan weddings for the past three weeks. My brother was going to strangle me soon if we didn't hire someone. And this person was going to be our last hope. As soon as she showed up, that was.

I looked down on my watch and tried to plan the rest of my day. I had thirty minutes to figure out what the hell was going on in the kitchen, and then I had to go to the meeting.

I nodded at a few guests who were sipping wine and eating a cheese plate and then at our innkeeper, Naomi. Naomi's honey-brown hair was cut in an angled bob that lit her face, and she grinned at me.

"Hello there, Boss Man," she whispered. "You might need to go to the kitchen."

"Do I want to know?" I asked with a grumble.

"I'm not sure. But I am going to go check in our

next guest, and then Elliott needs to meet with the Henderson couple."

"He'll be there." I didn't say that Elliot would rather chew off his own arm rather than deal with this, considering we had a family event coming in, one that Elliot was on target with planning. The wedding for next year was an important one, so we needed to work on it.

Naomi was a fantastic innkeeper, far more organized than any of us—and that was saying something since my brothers and I knew our way around schedules, to-do lists, and spreadsheets. Naomi was personable, smiled, and kept us on our toes.

Without her, I knew we wouldn't be able to do this. Hell, without Amos, our vineyard manager, I knew that Evan and Elijah wouldn't be able to handle the winery as they did. Naomi and Amos had come with the place when we had bought it, and I would be forever grateful that they had decided to stay on.

I gave Naomi another nod, then headed back to the kitchen and nearly walked right back out.

Tony stood there, a scowl on his face and his hands on his hips. "I don't understand what the fuck is wrong with this oven."

"What's going on?" I asked as Everett stood by

Tony. Everett was my quiet brother with usually a small smile on his face, only right then it looked like he was ready to scream.

I didn't know why Everett was even there since he was part responsible for the financials side of the company and usually worked with Elliot these days. Maybe he had come to the kitchen after the smell of burning as I had after Naomi's prodding.

Tony threw his hands in the air. "What's going on? This stove is a piece of shit. All of it is a piece of shit. I'm tired of this rustic place. I thought I would be coming to a Michelin star restaurant. To be my own chef. Instead, I have to make English breakfasts and pancakes with bananas. I might as well be at a bed and breakfast."

I pinched the bridge of my nose. "We're an inn, not a bed and breakfast."

"But I serve breakfast. That's all I do these days. That and cheese platters. Nobody comes for dinner. Nobody comes for lunch."

That was a lie. Tony worked for the winery and the retreat itself and served all the meals. But Tony wanted to go crazy with the menu, to try new and fantastical items that just weren't going to work here.

And I had a feeling I was going to throw up if I wasn't careful.

"I quit," Tony snapped, and I knew right then, it was done for. I was done.

"You can't quit," I growled while Everett held back a sigh.

"Yes, I can. I'm done. I'm done with you and this ranch. You're not cowboys. You're not even Texans. You're just people moving in on our territory." And with that, Tony stomped away, throwing his chef's apron on the ground.

I was thankful that the kitchen was on the other side of the library and front area, where most of the guests were if they weren't out on one of the tours of the area and city that Elliott had arranged for them. That was the whole point of this retreat. They could come visit, and could relax, or we could set them up on a tour of downtown San Antonio, or Canyon Lake, or any of the other places that were nearby.

And yet, Tony had just thrown a wrench into all of that. I didn't know what was worse, the smell of burning, Tony leaving, the water in the basement that wasn't truly a basement, or the fact that I was going to smell like charred food and wet jeans when I went to go meet this wedding planner.

"You're going to need to hire a new cook," Everett whispered.

I looked at my brother, at the man who did his best to make sure we didn't go bankrupt, and I wanted to just grumble. "I figured."

"I can help for now, but you know I'm only part-time. I can't stay away from my twins for too long," Sandy said as she came forward to take the pan off the stove. "I wish I could do full time, but this is all I can do for now."

Sandy had come back from maternity leave after we had already opened the retreat. She had been on with the former owners and was brilliant. But she had a right to be a mom and not want to work full time. I understood that, and I knew that Sandy didn't want to handle a whole kitchen by herself. She liked her position as a sous chef.

I was going to have to figure out what to do. Again.

"I'll get it done," I said while rubbing my temples.

"You know what we need to do," Everett whispered, and I shook my head.

"He'll kill us."

"Maybe, but it'll be worth it in the end. And speaking of, don't you have that interview soon? Or do you want me to take it?" His gaze tracked to my jeans.

I shook my head. "No, help Sandy."

Everett winced. "Just because I know how to slice an onion, it doesn't mean I'm good at cooking."

"I'm sorry, did you just say you could slice an onion? Get to it," Sandy put in with a smile, pointing at the sink. "Wash those hands."

"I cannot believe I just said that out loud. I just stepped right into it," Everett said with a sigh. "Go to the interview. You know what to ask."

"I do. And I hope we don't get screwed this time."

"You know, if we're lucky, we'll get someone as good as Roy's wedding planner, or at least that woman that we met. You know who she is." Everett grinned like a cat with the canary.

I narrowed my eyes. "Don't bring her up."

"Oh, I can't help it. A single dance, and you were drawn to her."

"What dance? You know what? No, I don't have time. We have to work on lunch and dinner. Tell me while you work," Sandy added with a wink.

Everett leaned toward her as he washed his hands. "Well, you see, there was this dance, and he met the perfect woman, and then she got engaged."

Sandy's eyes widened. "Engaged? How did that

happen? She was dating someone else?" she asked as she looked at me.

I pinched the bridge of my nose. "It was at Roy's place when we were looking at the venue to see if we wanted to buy the retreat here." I sighed, I knew if I just let it all out, she would move on from this conversation, and I would never have to deal with it again. "Somehow, I ended up at a wedding there, caught the garter. This woman caught the bouquet, and she happened to be the wedding planner. We danced, we laughed, and as she walked away, her boyfriend got down on one knee and proposed."

"No way!" She leaned forward with a fierce look on her face, her eyes bright. "What did she say?"

"I have no clue. I left." I ignored whatever feeling might want to show up at that thought. Everett gave me a glance, and I shook my head. "Enough of that. Yes, the wedding that she did was great, but I honestly have no idea who she is, and she has a job. She doesn't need to work here." And I didn't know what I would do if I saw her again or had to work with her. There had been such an intense connection that I knew it would be awkward as hell. But thankfully, she had her own business and wasn't going to come to the Wilder Retreat for a job.

I left Sandy and Everett on their own, knowing

that they were capable, at least for now. And I knew who we would have to hire if she said yes, and if my other brother didn't kill me first.

I washed my hands in the sink on the way out, grateful that at least I looked somewhat decent, if not a little disheveled, and made my way out front, hoping that the wedding planner who came in through the doors would be the one that would stick. Because we needed some good luck. After the day we've had, we needed some good luck.

I turned the corner and nearly tripped over my feet.

Because, of course, fate was this way.

It was her.

Of all the wedding planners from all the wedding venues, it was her.

**In the mood to read another family saga? Meet the Wilder Brothers in One Way Back to Me!**

# FROM ETCHED IN HONOR

## AUDREY

I dodged the blacked-tipped talons handily but nearly tripped over the wolf to my side. I winced as I jumped over Ronin and didn't let the fact that he cowered beside me insult my cat. After all, he was a new wolf. And he didn't know exactly how to fight yet. This wasn't exactly the training I had planned for the day, but there was no going back now, not when I needed to fight whatever these things were.

It looked like a man, a normal man, with excessive strength. Its eyes were dark-rimmed, but I couldn't see its irises to tell what color they were. And its fingernails had turned into claws, or perhaps the talons I had once thought. But they looked as if they had been dipped into black ink. The nails were black for sure, but even the fingertips seemed to radiate that darkness.

I had never seen the like, but as I was part of the Aspen Pack, I knew that not all was what it seemed, and there were many unknowns out there.

I let my claws push through my fingertips and raked the nails down the back of one. The man in front of me let out a shocked gasp, then fell to his knees. I didn't want any of that black tar or whatever it was to touch me. My cat didn't like the scent of it, and frankly, neither did the human part of me.

I was a lion shifter in the middle of a wolf Pack, a wolf Pack that was like none other.

And my cat already had enough and arched its back up.

There were two of these creatures in front of me, and they didn't scent of the rogues that we had been fighting for years, nor did they scent of wolf.

I wasn't sure if they were a witch gone bad or not, but whatever they were, we needed to deal with it before it was too late.

I grumbled a bit, then found a branch to toss at Ronin. Ronin gave me this odd look, his human face looking puzzled, and I sighed before I made sure he held the stick, and I pulled the dagger out of my boot.

I used my claws on the creature's back, but I wasn't about to get anywhere near its mouth.

My senses told me it wasn't a good idea, no matter what it was.

I used the dagger to stab the closest creature at the base of the skull and twisted. It let out a scream, one abruptly cutoff, before it fell to its knees, its body at an odd angle on the ground.

I went to the other one, but it came at Ronin quickly, ignoring me. I cursed under my breath, my cat ready to slice at those who endangered our people. Ronin was under our watch, and we refused to let him get hurt because we weren't strong enough.

I kept moving towards it, but Ronin smacked the thing with the branch.

Well, that was one way to fight it. Probably not the best way, but we were getting somewhere. At least I hoped so.

Ronin smacked it again, but then the creature gripped the branch and shook it. He tossed Ronin twenty feet back, and my brows winged up.

Well then, that was some strength. He probably

could even beat Hayes when it came to strength, and that polar bear was the strongest person I knew.

It seemed it was time for me to stop pussyfooting around, as it were, and take care of this thing.

It was bleeding from the claw marks, and the blood was red, so I counted that as something to take note of, but I wasn't sure what it meant.

I didn't want to wait to find out, so I moved forward and tossed my dagger directly into the creature's eyes.

It screamed, pulling at the dagger but not falling down.

That image would haunt my nightmares for years to come. Considering the number of things that already haunted my nightmares, that was saying something.

"Okay then. Why won't you die?"

"This is only the beginning," the creature growled as he pulled the dagger out of its eye.

I swallowed hard. I hadn't been aware it could talk. I had no idea what it was, but it wasn't dead from a dagger to the eye, and it stepped forward once, twice, and fell.

Oh good. It was dead. Thank the goddess because I wasn't sure exactly what I was supposed to do now.

I sighed and then went to take my dagger back.

Ronin sat on the ground and looked up at me before lowering his gaze.

His wolf was in the golden glow surrounding his iris, and my cat wanted to reach out, bat him on the head, and then hug him close.

Ronin wasn't submissive by any means, nor was he a paternal wolf. He was a dominant, but so in the middle of the chain that he could wobble either way depending on who was around him. And my cat was one of the most dominant shifters in the Pack.

It didn't matter that the rest of them were wolves except for a select few. My cat was Beta of the Aspen Pack and had held that title longer than any other leader within the Pack. Everyone else had gained their connection and responsibility after everything had changed.

I alone remained.

My heart ached, but I pushed away the pain.

Just because the rest of the hierarchy was relatively new in the past year and a half didn't mean we were falling or breaking.

I just happened to be the only one with experience.

Experience that was met with hatred in some eyes, but I was good at ignoring that.

I leaned down in front of Ronin and gripped the

back of his neck as I would a pup. He looked up at me then, meeting my gaze for an instant before lowering his eyes but not his chin.

My cat purred in happiness. That was showing who was more dominant, but not lowering. And that I counted as progress.

"Are you okay? Did their claws or teeth or anything else out of the ordinary touch you?"

Ronin shook his head. "No, I'm fine. I'm fine, but I messed up."

I shook my head. "Whatever that was, was far stronger than either one of us was prepared for."

He looked up at me then for just an instant and blinked in surprise. "You don't know what that was?"

I didn't want any more lies in my Pack, not after years of pain and sacrifice and nothing but lies. So I told him the truth. Chase would have to find his own path and tell me exactly what he wanted the rest of the Pack to know in general. After all, he was my Alpha and had once been my friend.

I pushed that thought away and squeezed the back of Ronin's neck again. The younger wolf relaxed marginally, and I knew he liked the action. "I don't know what that was. We're going to find out, though. It was strong, so strong that I had to use my dagger rather than my claws or strength. You did what you could, and while you aren't ready to hold a weapon on you at all times like that, we're getting there."

"I nearly tripped you," he grumbled.

"We were just finishing a long training session when those whatever they were slithered out of the trees as they did. They came on us out of nowhere, and we're both exhausted after our training."

He wrinkled his nose, and I knew he smelled the lie on that.

"Okay, you were exhausted. I'm tired. Does that make your wolf feel better?" I asked, putting a light-hearted note in my tone.

Ronin nodded. "Yes. Sorry. I'm still getting used to all these scents and everything."

My heart ached for him, and my cat wanted to reach out and lick his face just to make sure that he felt better. Doing that in human form with a new wolf, one that didn't know me well, was probably not the best thing.

"Everything's okay. We are going to figure out what these are and put them in the basement so that way our Healer can take a look at it."

"Maybe the other Packs know?"

That made me smile. "Hopefully, the others do. They've all dealt with many strange things."

"Well, we have our own strangeness," Ronin said with a bit of pride, and I felt it too. The Aspen Pack was unique in that we were not just wolves. Other than a few people who held our secrets, the rest of the world thought the only shifters out there were wolves. After all, they were the ones that had been forced to be revealed to the public. And after a war and scary end of times, humans and wolves lived in a decent harmony. The fact that the government had wolf sympathizers helped. Any scary laws that could have restricted the movements and freedoms of anyone magical in nature were now scrubbed off the table indefinitely.

Wolves and witches were able to live freely.

Cats and bears, on the other hand, were unheard of.

I knew of a couple of cats that roamed the earth as individuals, but I was the only lioness that I knew of near here other than Aimee. There was a lynx shifter as well, and she was my best friend, but other than that, it was just me here.

And there was only one bear that I knew of.

Perhaps there were other secret Packs that held them, and I had the hope in my heart that there were. But even most wolves didn't know we existed, and that had been for a reason years before.

Now I wasn't even sure what the reason could be.

I looked down at the two dead bodies next to me, my cat hissing, and ran my hand over Ronin's back. Then I stood up and helped him do the same.

"We should head back into the den, behind the wards. But we need to tell the others what happened."

There was no doubt that Chase as Alpha would be able to feel that something had indeed happened.

The others would as well since Steele was the Enforcer, and he could feel outside threats to the Pack. This just felt like such a different threat that I wasn't sure he would be able to tell what it was.

Cruz might be able to tell as well, but he was the Heir and felt so lost that I wasn't even sure he would know to respond at all. It didn't matter that he was a dominant wolf. We were all so far out of our depths, it was a little scary.

I rubbed at my chest and then was reminded again that I wasn't the only cat shifter around. At least the only lioness around. I wanted someone of my own kind, even if it didn't make sense. I should see Aimee. And check on her. She was a lioness like me because of what I had to do to save her.

I shook my head, remembering the Talon Pack lioness who now lived in a Pack of wolves as I did.

She was strong, mated to the Healer, and could handle anything on her own.

At least, that's what I figured. It wasn't like I could truly speak to her often these days, not with my needing to be with the Aspens as much as I was.

I turned to see Steele coming towards me, a glare on his face as always. I didn't know him well, though that was only because I had to hide my true loyalties for so long that I didn't know my Pack as I should.

He gave me a tight nod as he looked around at his lieutenants. "What happened here?"

I raised a brow because he wasn't as dominant as I was. The only person that was within this Pack was Chase, and even then, some days, it didn't feel like it.

Steele just shook his head, his own wolf understanding that he didn't get to growl at me like that in front of others. We were all still finding our place, figuring out how to work together as a cohesive unit. The fact that I hadn't had a cohesive unit with the previous hierarchy spoke volumes. We were taking our cues from the Redwoods and Talons. But even then, the Redwoods had decades of learning to work together and were an actual family. The hierarchy before the current generation was still around, guiding them. They weren't elders per se, but they were a tight unit.

The Talons, on the other hand, had to rebuild from the ground up at one point, and so we were trying to follow their lead. Much like the Central Pack was doing. Though their Pack had been completely demolished, only coming back with a blessing from the actual moon goddess, the goddess of wolves.

I shook my head and looked over at Steele. "I don't know. I'm trying to figure it out myself."

I explained about the dark claws and the fact that it had spoken even after we had shoved a dagger into its eye. Steele raised a brow, then pulled out his phone. "We should talk with the Redwoods and the Talons. They might have seen something when they were down south."

I frowned, then remembered that nearly a year ago the Tracker for the Redwood Pack had gone down south to meet another Pack of all things and had come up with something similar. The dark smudges and black bite marks.

"Do you think it's that? I thought that those were genetically modified rogues or whatever that they had found."

"Not exactly. The dead bodies that piled up

happened to be because of that rogue, the wolf that had gotten out thanks to the drug that is no longer a problem within our borders. However, the black marks seemed to be something different."

I cursed under my breath. "I didn't know that."

"I only think I know it because I was talking with Gina."

Gina was the Enforcer of the Redwood Pack, his counterpart, and had more experience than he did, but only barely.

"Okay. I'll talk with Chase then. Do you guys have this settled?"

"We do. We'll meet up with Wren."

A smile slid over my face at the mention of my best friend's name. Wren was a lynx shifter and our Healer.

As long as she was connected to the Pack, she could use those bonds to heal those around her. She was also an MD and kept up with her medical studies throughout her years. She had been a doctor before the goddesses had called on her to become the Healer of our Pack. It had fit, and now she worked on the mystical side and the medical side.

"Hopefully, she'll figure it out, and hey, I hear there's a new geneticist joining the Pacific Northwest Pack Alliance."

I grinned. "Is that the name that you're going with now?" I asked.

Steele rolled his eyes. "I think Cruz is having a little too much fun with the other Packs forming names. But since we're working so close together, the Pacific Northwest Pack Alliance seems to be working with the four of us."

That made me smile because it wasn't just the Redwoods and the Talons any longer. The Aspens were going to bring things to the table, and I knew the Centrals were doing the same. Even though the Centrals had a dark past with the Redwoods, we had just as much of a dark one with the Talons.

My stomach ached at that thought, and my cat scratched at me, so I pushed that thought away and sighed. "I need to go meet with Chase."

"I take it training's over then?" he asked, looking at Ronin.

Ronin lowered his head, and if he were in wolf form, his tail would've been tucked between his legs. I moved forward, went on my tiptoes, and ran my hand through his hair. "You're fine. We'll finish up the day after tomorrow. I know you have your studies."

The kid, and he really was a kid, only in his early twenties, beamed at me. "Yes, true. Thank you so much for your help. I know I'm getting better, right?"

"You are. You fought well today. We weren't expecting this, but we made it out because we had each other. So thank you."

His eyes widened before he walked away, speaking with another wolf his age that was a Lieutenant. That Lieutenant was far stronger in dominance but had just an edge of maternal nature to her that she seemed to ease Ronin's wolf.

"You're good with him."

I looked at Steele. "I'm trying. Sometimes I feel like I have no idea what I'm doing."

He swallowed hard. "I feel like that too. Even though you've been Beta for longer, you had to be a different Beta before."

I knew he'd said it as a compliment, but it felt like a slap nonetheless. "I know. But we have new wolves joining the Pack every week, it seems."

"We do. And that's something that Chase is going to want to talk to you about," he added with a grimace.

"What?"

"Allister's here."

I blinked at his mention of the Thames Pack Alpha. The Thames Pack was over by the actual

Thames River in England. "I didn't realize he was visiting."

"He wanted to meet with our alliance, or whatever else he wants to call it. And in doing so, he brought with him a lone wolf that's been with them for a while but wanted to come back to the United States. And since the Centrals and the Aspens are pretty much recruiting for Pack members at this point, he figured this guy would work out well with us."

"Oh. Okay. What does it have to do with me?"

"As Beta, Chase wants you to help him get acclimated to the den. He's going to blood him in later today."

"Him? Just one?"

"There are two women that are joining the Central Pack, from what I can tell. But we get the Tracker."

My lion perked up, her tail swishing back and forth. "He's a Tracker?"

"He is, and has the talent for it, and since our Pack doesn't actually have one as part of the hierarchy, Chase says the moon goddess will bestow the new guy with the title."

A Tracker was someone who could follow the Pack lines and use extrasensory abilities to find anyone within the Pack. If magic or other impediments were in the way, it didn't always work, but a Tracker was great to have. We hadn't had one in a decade. Not since our former Alpha had killed him for daring to disobey him.

I swallowed hard, thinking of another Tracker that I'd met in my lifetime. One I didn't want to think about too hard because it hurt even to imagine.

"I guess since I'm the Beta, it's my job to see to the needs of the Pack."

Steele saluted me as he turned back to work with the dead bodies that I had left behind, and I shook my hair out before making my way towards the den.

The den was situated in the northern part of California, amongst the Redwood trees, much like the Redwood namesake Pack that was a little more north of us. We took over Washington, Oregon, and California once you put all of the Pack territories together. We were a large group, but insular.

Our wards protected the den itself, but a lot of our Pack lived outside the den, within the communities of humans and witches. That was how it should be. A den was a place to come home to.

It hadn't been like that for so long that it almost

felt odd to think that now this den could be healthy once again.

I walked through the wards, past the sentries, and let the magic settle over my skin. My cat preened, enjoying the tingles of magic, and I shook my head at it.

Silly cat.

She wanted to run, to let the world look at her glorious golden pelt, but I ignored her. We had things to do. We could laze in the sun later.

I turned the corner, my cat perking up, an odd scent hitting her nose.

I frowned, wondering why it scented so familiar.

"Audrey. You're here. Good," Chase, my Alpha, stated as I came towards him, but my heart stuttered, my skin breaking out into a cold sweat. I couldn't focus. Not on him.

It couldn't be.

This wasn't him.

It was a ghost, a death. This was nothing. I was dreaming. Maybe I had been bitten by whatever I just fought, and now I was dead.

Because this couldn't be true.

"Audrey, you know Allister, and this is Gavin. He'll be a new member of the Aspen Pack."

*Gavin.* That was the name of the stranger, the stranger with the eyes.

This wasn't Gavin.

No, the man before me was the replica of Basil.

My mate.

My dead mate.

**Meet the Aspen Pack with Etched in Honor!**

# FROM BREATH AND RUIN

## AN ELEMENTS OF FIVE ROMANTASY

The dreams didn't come often, but when they did, it usually took me far too long to realize I could find my way out of them. At least, *most* of the time, I could make my way out. Other times, no matter how hard I tried to shake myself awake or tear at the seams of what the dream could be, I was forced to live within them, in the nightmares that felt far too real.

My heartbeat thudded in my ears as I tried to get my bearings once again. The dreams were never the same in what happened or even where I was when they occurred, but there was a thread that seemed familiar, as if it were calling to me in a way I could never understand.

Sometimes, I was on the fringe, watching the

court of royals dance and hide their daggers of both wit and steel. Then they'd bow and turn to smoke, the ashes of their lies and hidden admissions blowing away like dust in the wind.

Other times, I was in the middle of the action, hurtling from side to side as towers fell, and water rushed by. Air blew through my hair, whipping it into my face, the earth below me trembling as fire rained down on all of us.

Tonight, however, the visions weren't either of those. Yes, I was in the present, the dream happening to me rather than me being a witness to an absolution I would never understand.

But I stood in a clearing, winter on my back, summer facing me down with wicked heat. Spring danced along my right side with a cool warmth that didn't make sense, while fall brushed my left, its warming coolness confusing me even further.

There were two shadows in front of me, their arms outstretched, each calling my name in whispers. I could only hear their breaths, not their voices, so I had no idea who they were or what they represented in this dream that I knew would linger long after I woke.

"Lyric," they called in unison.

"Lyric."

And though that was my name, it still didn't sound as if they were truly calling to me. Instead, it was as if they called to the person they needed me to be. I wasn't that person, though. Wasn't what they needed, and I knew I may not ever be.

And while I still had the same body shape as I did when I was awake—my slightly larger-than-average curves filling out my dress, and my height just below average so the bottom of my hem slid along the mud —I wasn't truly *me* in the dream.

My blond hair blew in the wind, catching the light and making it look white at times, gold at others. The shade was always changing depending on how much sun I took in during the season, but in this dream, it changed with the direction I turned.

*It isn't truly me,* I told myself again. This wasn't my dress, this wasn't my life.

Those shadows couldn't actually call to me because I *wasn't me.*

"Lyric," the shadows called again.

"Wake up," the one nearest the spring side demanded.

"It's time," the one closest to fall whispered.

And though they were both whispers, they sounded like screams in my ear.

I jolted awake, my sweat-slick skin clammy as I

tried to catch my breath. My tank was soaked, sticking to my body, and my shorts had ridden up as if I'd thrashed in my sleep. Considering my comforter was on the floor, and my sheet was currently a knot at the end of my bed, I would say that was probably exactly what had happened.

I swallowed hard, narrowing my eyes at the clock, trying to see what time it was. The sun was already up, even though it wasn't quite seven in the morning, but it was summer in Denver, Colorado, and that meant blue skies, bright sun, and the occasional rain that came out of nowhere.

I had my white curtains drawn, but they didn't really block out the light, so I'd learned to sleep through the rays on my face long ago. I had to if I ever wanted to sleep in. And since I was also a teenager, sleeping in was part of life—especially during the summer.

I might be eighteen, out of high school and ready to start college in the fall, but I still felt like the teenager who wanted to sleep in and not have to wake up early for classes. It didn't help that my walls were still a light lilac from when I'd been in my purple phase, and there was still lace on my curtains and the skirt of my bed.

My family made a decent income, but we were

firmly in the middle of middle class, and these days, that meant there wasn't money to update my bedroom to something a little less tween girl and a little more college-bound woman. I didn't care too much, however. I wasn't staying here long. Soon, I'd be in a dorm at the local university, an offshoot of the University of Colorado since there was no way I could afford Boulder's campus. Plus, this way, I could still be close to home.

Because as much as I might think I was ready to start my new life and be an adult, the nightmares that had plagued me for as long as I could remember told me that I wasn't as grown-up as I thought.

Honestly, what kind of teenager still needed a nightlight because she was scared of the shadows?

Me, apparently. Lyric Camaron, the walking embodiment of indecision and someone not quite ready for anything.

I ran a hand over my face, holding back a gag at how sweaty I was, and let out a sigh. The dreams hadn't happened so often before, but now they came almost every other night, and I had no idea what they meant. I'd always had a vivid imagination, but my dreams took that to a whole new level.

I wasn't a little girl anymore, and yet I still dreamed of princes and princesses, of magic and might. I dreamed of courts and pretty dresses, and flowers and rain. Still, I thought that was probably all just a front for what the dreams actually carried. A veil across the hate and lies and mystery of everything that came with them.

I'd always secretly wanted to write them down, to make them into a book or just a few stories, but for some reason, I'd held myself back. There was no use documenting what never made sense. The dreams scared me even when they shouldn't, and writing them down would only make them more real.

And it wasn't like writing would help me in my real life outside of the dreams. I needed to grow up, stop thinking about fairy tales that weren't bright and shiny, and figure out what I wanted to be when I grew up. Because I wasn't a little kid anymore and, sadly, the time to make those choices had already started to pass me by, and I was struggling to keep up.

"Shut up, Lyric," I mumbled to myself. It was far too early, and I still wasn't awake enough for my mind to be going down that path. I'd likely be getting a very similar lecture from my parents over breakfast—and perhaps lunch and dinner—as it was.

They loved me, and I loved them.

And that meant I needed to be a better daughter.

The first step to doing that was getting out of bed and washing off the sweat that coated my skin. Then, I'd wash my sheets, air out my comforter, and maybe even go for a run so I could get the cobwebs out of my mind. I wasn't a coffee fan since I tended to need far too much sugar to even like it, so I couldn't have a cup of that to help. So, that meant chores and fresh air so I could get out of my funk, let the dreams lie where they needed to be—far from my reality—and get on with my day.

I could do that. Totally. If only I could get the images from the dream out of my mind.

Those two shadows had been in more than one of my nightmares, and I couldn't help but think that they meant something. Who or what did they represent? Why were they important? I didn't know if they were male or female or if they were truly people at all. If they were supposed to be love interests, then having them be either a man or a woman would only mean that my dream-self represented my real-self since I was attracted to both and had dated both in real life. But I still didn't know what the dreams or the shadows in them really meant.

In a few, the apparitions had moved, and I could almost imagine them wanting to be even closer.

They always held out their hands, as if I had to make a decision between them, to go to one or the other.

The seasons coming at me all at once seemed like another symbol for choice and change, as well. The same with the instances where I was covered in earth or water, air or flame. All of it indicated choice.

So maybe the dreams didn't mean anything beyond what I already knew.

It was time for me to make a choice.

A choice regarding who I could be—who Lyric Camaron would be as an adult.

That choice seemed the hardest of all, and yet I knew it was important. All teenagers went through this, they all had to make decisions, no matter what course outside forces wanted them to take.

I knew there was a path laid out before me, one that would lead to a life not unlike the one I held now, one made of decisions that made practical sense. That was the one I knew I should take, the one that would be easier and yet far more thought-out.

And yet part of me wanted something different. I wanted to be a Lyric who wasn't so middle-of-the-road as I currently was as a bisexual teenager living in Denver, Colorado.

There were choices I had to make. Clear-cut ones that had nothing to do with royals and elements, nothing to do with seasons and change.

I would make the right choice.

I had to.

And I would ignore the dreams and the idea that there could be something more for me. There hadn't been before, and I wasn't going to lie in wait for answers that scared me, translations of dreams that challenged me.

I would make my own way, make my own choices.

And they would be the right ones because they would be *mine*.

The dreams would go away eventually.

They would fade just like the young girl I used to be. In its place would be the future I needed, the one I craved.

I told myself I wouldn't dream again. I couldn't.

Because I didn't want to know what those shadows meant. I didn't want to know why they knew my name.

I didn't want to know why it all felt so real. And, above all else, I didn't want to know why I saw those same shadows when I was awake. Because those were the ones that scared me. The ones that were far too real.

I was Lyric, the girl with everything to look forward to. I wasn't the girl who saw shadows, who had dreams.

I couldn't be.

**Meet Lyric and the Romantasy series that brings the power of secrets and choices. Two princes. One to save them all. Find out more in From Breath and Ruin!**

# FROM DAWN UNEARTHED

## A RAVENWOOD COVEN NOVEL

age

I SQUINTED AS I LOOKED AT THE GPS, TRYING TO make sense of the directions. I had been across the Pennsylvania border for over an hour now, and I needed to find the right exit that would take me off the main highway and onto one of the many smaller roads that encompassed Pennsylvania. I needed to get to my new home, or at least what others would have me call my new home. I still wasn't quite sure what that would mean as of yet.

My hands clenched the steering wheel, and I told myself everything would be okay. I was making a dramatic move, with even more unknown changes to come, but it was for a purpose.

Because Ravenwood, Pennsylvania called to me.

I shook my head, frowning at myself as I checked the next exit.

The town wasn't calling to me. That was preposterous. Towns didn't reach out to people. And I did my best to ignore the odd whispers in my head, the pull to a place I'd never been to nor even thought of before. I pushed away the idea of a shadow person filling my vision. I wasn't being pulled toward anyone either. That was silly. The only people I knew in Ravenwood were my aunt and Rowen, who had sold me the building where I was setting up my business. Ravenwood was a place. Somewhere I would make my new home.

I couldn't go back to where I had been for so many years. I couldn't rebuild my life from the ashes in a place that still sparked with embers of sorrow and pain. I did my best to empty those thoughts from my mind because they wouldn't help anyone.

I was moving to a new place, in a new state, to a new home.

Ravenwood was a small town north of Philadelphia, and one I had only heard of because my aunt lived there. If asked to name cities in Pennsylvania, most people wouldn't even think of the town. She owned a small bookshop called Ravenwood Pages and frequently spoke of the warmth radiating through the town and how everybody was welcome.

Rupert and I had always meant to come north from Norfolk, Virginia, where we had lived for the entirety of our marriage, but things had never worked out. Between work, our conflicting plans, and life in general, we hadn't been able to visit my aunt Penelope at her bookshop. Looking back, I didn't know why. It wasn't as if it was too far of a drive—not when it meant seeing my aunt in her home. Now that I thought about it more, it felt as if something had been pushing us away. And, once again, that was an odd thought to have.

My aunt usually came down to visit us for holidays, or we went to Rupert's family's place. I last saw Penelope after the funeral when she came to make sure I was okay. Not that I could *be* okay. Nothing about losing one's husband at twenty-four years old was okay.

Everyone kept saying that we had our entire lives before us, that they couldn't wait to see what would happen between Rupert and me. They wanted us to thrive, have babies, and create a whole family in our Virginia town. That hadn't happened. No, nothing had happened the way it should have. Rupert was gone. And so quickly, I could barely even pause to catch my breath.

A brain tumor had taken him before I'd even had a chance to come to terms with the idea that I might lose my husband. Now, he was gone, leaving nothing for me. Not his family, nor the rest of mine. Rupert's family hadn't wanted anything to do with me after Rupert died. They saw my pain *and* theirs etched onto my face every time they looked at me and had pushed me away because of it.

Now, I was on the long road to a new beginning, one where I needed to stop feeling the melancholy stretching over me, digging its claws into my flesh as I struggled to cope.

I shook away my thoughts, doing my best to breathe. That was all I needed to do. Breathe.

My dash lit up, and the sound of an incoming phone call filled the car. My lips turned up into a small smile as I saw the readout and answered.

"Aunt Penelope," I said softly, waiting for the next exit as I kept my attention on the road.

"Are you almost here?" she asked, her voice warm, soothing. She was always that way, as if every time I was near her, she infused me with warmth and magic. Not real magic, of course. Though my mother joked that my aunt was a witch, I knew that wasn't the case.

Magic didn't exist.

And, once again, here I was having odd thoughts.

"I'm almost there. I think it's the next exit."

My aunt was silent for a moment before she spoke again. "Take the exit and make sure you stay on the path. Don't take a detour or stop for anything that might come your way. Ravenwood is waiting for you."

I frowned, looking at the GPS again. "What do you mean?" Her words were weird. Then again, everything I'd been thinking for the past hour had been strange.

Another pause. "Nothing, darling. You'll be here soon. Finally. And Ravenwood will welcome you home. As will I."

"I hope so," I muttered as tension rolled over me again at the momentous changes I was barreling through. "Are we sure you need a bakery? It's a small town. There has to be one already."

"There was one a few years ago, but the tenants moved on. Lately, we've been dealing with the supermarket and their baked goods. Not that they aren't adequate, but there's nothing like bread and sweet treats from a true bakery. From *your* bakery.

The town needs you, Sage. The building is ready and outfitted to your specifications. You'll be able to start soon."

My stomach clenched, but I still smiled. I hadn't made it up to Ravenwood yet because I had been dealing with estate issues and Rupert's family. Closing up my life and my house back in Norfolk while trying to open a bakery and a small business in a town I had never even been to, had been all-consuming. I still couldn't believe I was doing it, but things were falling into place.

Maybe they needed to after everything else had shattered around me. Grief wrapped its spindly fingers around my throat, squeezing, suffocating, the mere force of it overwhelming.

"It will be good to see you," I said, my voice choked.

"I can't wait to hold you again, my Sage. See you soon, darling. Remember, stay on the path and you'll find Ravenwood."

She hung up, and I frowned. "That was peculiar," I whispered. Though Aunt Penelope was pretty unusual. She was always giving advice, her voice filled with warmth and wisdom when she did.

She wanted me to come *home*. Such an incongruous word. Because I had thought I'd had a home for so long. Yet, now, it was gone. There was nothing for me back in the small house where I'd loved Rupert. Nothing for me in Virginia at all.

Rupert was gone, and all ties I had to that life had faded away with him, or perhaps they'd been snapped into pieces by the agony. The brain tumor had taken him quickly, even as he wasted away. I never wanted that image in my head again, even in the short years since I had lost him.

I loved him, and I would always love him, but I was ready to move on now. I'd spent these past couple of years finding out who I was. I needed to discover who I could be without him and outside of the place that held our memories.

I had gone through my grief differently than most. And I wasn't the same person I had been before. I was finding my way—a home to settle in.

Maybe that was healing. I didn't know, but I would find out. I needed to. And whatever pulled me toward Ravenwood urged me to do so.

My GPS signaled, and I took the next exit.

Ravenwood beckoned me.

I crossed over the exit and got onto the road, the same path my aunt had just mentioned. As soon as I did, dark clouds filled the sky. I frowned and looked up, wondering where the storm had come from. I hadn't known there was a storm on the horizon. I hadn't seen it, but maybe I hadn't been paying enough attention—which probably wasn't smart, considering I was still driving, and it had been a long day.

A long month. A long few years. A long agony.

I frowned and shook my head as the rain began splattering on the windshield. I quickly turned on the wipers, the sound almost…rusty. It hadn't rained in a while.

"This storm came out of nowhere," I muttered.

I hadn't remembered seeing it on my weather app that morning when I left, but storms did pop up here. Maybe this was the usual. I didn't know. I didn't know anything about Ravenwood. Other than the fact that my aunt had told me to come.

And since I had nothing else to do, I went. Now here I was, entering this small town as lightning streaked overhead, cracking in the sky. I swallowed hard, my knuckles going white as I kept on the road.

The rain began beating down harder, so loud that I could barely hear my thoughts. I had long since turned the radio down, and all I could hear was the sound of the storm raging outside. One I hadn't even seen until it surrounded me.

Dark clouds burst overhead, the rain becoming a

deluge. The road was so slick that I was afraid I might need to pull off, but I didn't know where to do that. Would other cars be able to see me? My lights were on bright, even in the middle of the day, but I could barely see. It was as if night had come out of nowhere.

I swallowed hard, sensing the taste of metal on my tongue as fear encroached.

I needed to focus, to get through this. I had to find a place to pull off. There was nowhere, other than the embankment, and that didn't seem safe. I needed to find my way to a part of the road to pause, collect myself, and hopefully let the storm pass. And then I could get to my aunt and Ravenwood. The wind rattled my car, and I nearly skidded off the road.

"Crap," I whispered and slowed down. There weren't any other cars, no lights, and I had no idea where I was. I looked at the GPS, but all I saw was darkness. It couldn't seem to find me in the storm. None of this made any sense.

I looked up and screamed, slamming on the brakes even though I knew that was a stupid move in this rain.

A dark wolf stood in front of me, its eyes glowing

gold in the headlights. I shouted, hoping to hell I didn't hit him.

I spun, fishtailing on the wet road, and did my best to steer into the skid, but I couldn't remember what direction that was. Was I supposed to go with my back wheels or my front wheels? All thoughts of driver's ed, and everything I had ever learned about driving through a storm escaped me. Tires screeched. I saw the eyes of the wolf again, and it lifted its lip, baring one fang.

I blinked as if lost in the moment. Everything froze around me, and warmth suffused me as I tried to focus. Attempted to see what was going on.

The wolf looked at me. When I blinked again, it was gone.

Everything moved quickly after that, and I was silent as I kept my hands on the wheel, trying not to roll over or skid off into the dirt and grass along the side of the highway, but there was no stopping my car.

The wet road, my overreaction, the storm, and that wolf had created this.

My car skidded horizontally through the grass, and the sound of my wheels popping as I slammed into the grass to the side echoed in my mind, nearly deafening me.

I blinked, my mouth dry as I tried to keep myself steady.

I was going to die. I wasn't even going to make it to my new home. I would die on this road with nobody around.

I would be alone. After so much time wondering who I could be as someone standing on their own two feet, I would die alone.

Finally, my car stopped, and I tried to breathe, my heart beating so fast I could practically hear it beating a staccato rhythm in my skull.

I quickly looked around and then looked down at myself.

There wasn't a scratch on me. I was fine. My car, on the other hand…I didn't know.

I couldn't see anything in front of me, not even the front of the car. Was I supposed to turn off my engine? I should call someone. I needed to do something. I looked down at my phone and cursed.

No signal.

Did Ravenwood have no cell service?

Someone had to come along soon. Though I needed to do something other than sit here. Someone would come and help me. Or maybe I could walk through the storm and find my way to help. No, I should stay in my warm car and then move towards the town once the storm let up.

That was the smart thing, right?

I looked through the window at the fallen tree in front of me and let out a relieved breath. If I had skidded a foot more, I would have hit it, and I could have died. The branches were sharp. It would have likely punctured the window and me.

Somehow, I hadn't hit that directly. I had to count that as a win.

I looked up the path once more and froze. A man lay under the tree. I couldn't be seeing this right. But *somebody* was there.

I pulled out my phone, even though it was a brick at this point, and scrambled for the door. It might be raining, and it could be a serial killer for all I knew, but I couldn't sit there and watch him practically drown in the mud. What if he was alive? What if he was hurt? I needed to find a way to help him.

My boots slid in the mud as I made my way towards the fallen man under the tree.

"Excuse me?" I asked over the rain, my voice shaking. "Hello?"

No answer. I knew that was stupid. It wasn't like he would answer if he was passed out or worse. I swallowed hard and moved forward before I knelt beside the man. His back rose and fell with his breaths, and I saw blood on his head from a small gash.

He was alive, though I knew I shouldn't move him. What if he had hurt his back? I didn't know *what* I was supposed to do.

I leaned forward and slowly brushed my fingertips across his forehead toward his temple.

He had a big beard, strong cheekbones, and a furrowed brow. His dark hair was slicked back, wet from the rain, and splattered with mud. He looked so strong, a little intimidating, but was passed out and clearly hurt.

I didn't know how to help. Yet something screamed inside of me to at least try. To pull him back and attempt to save him. I'd never felt this way before, and I wasn't sure I liked it. I could barely breathe. I needed to help this man. I needed to do something.

"Excuse me?" I whispered again and brushed his skin with my fingertips once more.

Shock slid up my body and slammed into my arm. I fell back hard into the mud and scrambled away from him. He looked up at me suddenly, blinking, his eyes a dark brown ringed with a bright gold that seemed to shine in the low light the storm allowed.

He huffed out a breath and growled.

An actual growl.

Then I looked at his eyes again. They were no longer brown. They'd turned fully gold.

Just like the wolf I had seen.

That wasn't right. It couldn't be. I was seeing things. I had hit my head harder than I thought, and this was all a dream. A delusion. Because I didn't feel right. Not with something pulsating inside me: the sudden urge to reach out and touch this man, make sure he was real.

Lightning struck so close, it popped my ears. I let out a squeak. The man beneath the tree growled, cursed under his breath, and then slowly made his way out from under the large branches.

"You shouldn't...you shouldn't do that. You could be hurt." I wanted to reach out and touch him again, to help him. Something inside me pushed me forward, made me want to tell him that everything would be okay as I wrapped my arms around him.

I pushed away that strange urge.

"I'm fine," he growled. He tilted his head as he studied me, his nostrils flaring. "It seems you're the one who saved me."

"What?" I asked, my entire body shaking with warmth and shock. I really couldn't breathe. What was going on?

He reached out as if to touch me, then let his hand fall. I wanted to move forward but I couldn't. We both sat there staring at each other as if we were the only two people in the world in a middle of a storm. It didn't make any sense. "It's okay, little witch. I think you shocked the hell out of me, but I'm awake now and fine. We should get out of this storm."

I scrambled away, my eyes wide. *Little witch*? Why had he called me that? I looked down at my hands and nearly shrieked again, but I had no breath left in me. It looked as if lightning scorched up my arm, white lines of power sliding up to my chest and down my sides.

My hips ached and burned. I scrambled for my shirt, lifting it. The man in front of me raised his brows and met my gaze.

"You okay?" He moved forward this time, his voice a deep growl of anger and... possession?

I shook my head, tried to catch my breath. As if waking from a dream, I realized that what I'd thought was real seemed to be wrong.

My memories were realigning, and I couldn't

make sense of them. Part of me remembered waking up with inked abstract fish and waves across my hips in a belt when I was younger. I hadn't known why I'd gotten the tattoo. I didn't remember sitting for the artist, but I'd told myself that I had done it because tattoos didn't appear out of nowhere. Rupert had never liked it, but it had been *mine*. It had called to me, and I knew I needed it. It didn't make any sense. Only now, I remembered the truth. I'd woken up one day with my body inked in this anchor to…something as if I'd been meant to have it.

Why had I thought I'd gone into a shop and requested it?

*Maybe because that was the rational answer.*

Only there was nothing sane about what I saw now.

The waves thrashed against my hips, moving around my body as if in a current. The fish swam in and out of the waves, breaking through the water and then diving back in.

Maybe I *had* hit my head.

*My tattoo is moving.*

The man looked at me and then over my shoulder. "I'm fine," he said, but he wasn't talking to me.

I turned to where he was looking, and my mouth dropped open, a scream ready. Then whatever had been pulsating within me, whatever hallucination arced through my brain, hit me again. I fell, my head splashing into the mud. I heard the man in front of me growl again, mumbling a curse as he reached for me.

All I could think about was the creature behind me. The large brown bear that I hadn't noticed before. I was sure it would finish me off if the burning that sliced through my body didn't do it first.

And then...there was nothing.

Nothing but questions.

And wrongness.

And darkness.

**Read the rest in Dawn Unearthed! Are you ready for more fated mates?**